Day
by
Day

N.C. Jones

PAGE PUBLISHING, INC.
Conneaut Lake, PA

First originally published by Page Publishing 2020

Edited by Chris Roush

ISBN 978-1-6624-1801-3 (pbk)
ISBN 978-1-6624-1802-0 (digital)

Printed in the United States of America

CONTENTS

——————— ACKNOWLEDGMENTS ———————

I am thankful for the support of my family.

My husband, Jeff.

My daughter, Heather, and her family: Chad, Nolan, Eli.

My son, Andy, and his family: Cassie, Raylan, Elliott.

A special thanks to Chris Roush for all his help.

CHAPTER 1

Kaitlyn

Oh my god! Where am I!

Katie woke to find herself in a dark room—*not hers!* As she rubbed her eyes, she tried to figure out where she was. The last thing she remembered she was helping a little girl with her puppy.

Kaitlyn O'Connor lived her whole life in Albuquerque, New Mexico. After graduating high school the previous year, her parents had treated her with a cruise. Upon her return, after seeing all the cruelty in the world, she decided to help the needy. She was to start college that fall, ready to fulfill that dream.

Katie's dad and mom, Joseph and Margaret O'Connor, owned the sporting-goods store in town, O'Connor's Fish and Game. The store had been open for many years. Generation after generation the store prospered. It started out in the garage of Joseph's grandfather twenty miles outside Albuquerque. When Joseph's father took over, he moved it to a two-story block house downtown. Downstairs were the fishing rods with all the accessories, along with all kinds of hunting supplies: rifles, shotguns, and muzzle loaders with an abundance of ammo for the adults; BB guns and traps for the younger kids. Upstairs held a small assortment of clothing. When Joseph took over, he brought the store into the twenty-first century. He built a huge all-on-one-floor store; a beautiful log building located at the end of town. He organized the inventory: clothing in front, a fishing department and gun department toward the back. He also added handguns. O'Connor Fish and Game was now worldwide, having its regular walk in customers, but most of the profits came in from catalog and online orders.

Katie and Charlie, her boyfriend, dated for over two years. They each had their dreams. She was going to college; he wanted to stay home, marry Katie, and have a family, all while working with his father in the family excavating business. He knew of her plans and tried to understand by letting her follow that dream. All they did was argue when she got home from her cruise. He wanted to spend time with her, but she had other things on her mind: to start helping others. On Saturdays Katie went from house to house, collecting clothing and other essentials that were no longer needed by her neighbors. She also went to the surrounding towns, collecting items for the shelters. On Sundays Katie worked both lunch and dinner at the homeless shelters, dedicating all her time in helping the unfortunate. Charlie and Katie drifted further and further apart until they finally went their separate ways.

Jack and Madeline Hayes and their daughter, Jackie, lived near the Sandia Mountains, some thirty miles from Albuquerque. They were surrounded by miles and miles of desert. Jack, thirty-six, worked as little as possible, just enough to put food on the table, pay a few bills, and of course, purchase his favorite bottle. He drank a lot. Always down on his luck, he vainly waited for his ship to come in. Maddy, his wife of eleven years, looked older than her age of twenty-seven. Having lost her previous baby a year ago, she had never regained her strength or the will to live. Having just moved to this new home, Maddy found herself pregnant. This new life she was carrying gave her new hope in their marriage, praying every night for it to be the son Jack wanted. Often, when Jack came home in the evenings from work, he would be enraged when things did not go his way. If something wasn't right at home, he let his fists do all the talking. The receiver of those fists was always Maddy. Many nights she went to bed with blackened eyes. Three months into the pregnancy, from all the beatings, she lost the baby. It was the little boy that she had so desperately wanted.

What kept her going was Jackie, her little girl. Jack never let her forget losing that baby. "It's your fault. You killed my son!" he would shout at her. He failed to remember it was his beatings that caused her to lose the child. After that happened, she did not care about keeping up with the day-to-day cleaning around the house and cooked very little. Maddy mostly stayed in their bedroom, leaving little Jackie trying to fix the meals. She was only ten years of age and did the best she could. Jack had not touched his wife sexually in over a year. Jackie attended Route 66 elementary school in Edgewood some eleven miles away. She was never allowed to play with any friends from school or invite anyone home. She was only allowed to attend school and then come straight home. She had only herself because of her father.

One Sunday morning Jack sat at the table, expecting breakfast. Jackie took her daddy toast and a cup of coffee. The toast was burnt black, and the coffee was thick as molasses. Taking a drink, he spit it all over the table.

Looking at his daughter, "What the hell is this?" he yelled as he threw the cup against the wall. The broken pieces scattered all over the floor, and coffee splattered the wall. Glaring at his wife sitting in the next room, he asked, "Is it asking too much to get a decent cup of coffee? Can't you do anything?"

Jackie, looking down, and started to cry, "I'm sorry! I'm sorry!" and ran to her room.

Grabbing his hat and what money there was, Jack stormed out, shouting, "I'm going to town! You'll see me when you see me!"

Wheels squealing, he drove off.

As soon as Joseph got home on Monday after work, he went straight to his daughter's room.

"Katie, I need you…" Seeing her on the phone, he immediately stopped talking.

Katie held up her finger, saying, "Libby, can I call you back?" Hanging up the phone, she asked, "Dad, what were you about to say?"

"I forgot Joan is off this week, and I need help two to three days."

"Dad! You know I was planning to go with Libby into town to finish shopping. We were going to get a room and just hang out a few days. Our last time together before college."

"You have plenty of time, this being the middle of July. You still have all of August before registration in September. Tell you what! If you help me all next week, I will treat you and a few friends to do your shopping in Santa Fe. Three nights away from here to whoop it up and shop till you drop. I'll even throw in that Apple laptop you've been drooling all over. How about it?"

"You mean it, Dad!" Jumping up, she hugged her father. "You got a deal!" Picking up the phone, she dialed Libby back. "Sorry, Lib, our plans have changed. I'm needed at the store. We can go in a couple weeks, and I have great news. Santa Fe for three nights, and Dad is paying!"

"Katie, can you help me out here few minutes? Go ahead and unlock the doors."

Stepping out, Katie looked around town. Would she miss being here? What if she wouldn't fit in at school? Shaking her head, she put all those thoughts to the back of her mind and went back in to start her day.

Jack stumbled out the door of his friend's house and saw Katie in front of the store. Taking another swig from his bottle, he wiped his mouth and stared.

"Gosh, dang! I'd like to get some of that!"

Fred Gates, his friend of many years, lived at the end of town across the street from the O'Connor's store. Hearing Jack talking, he came out and asked, "Man, who you talking to?" before he spotted Katie. "You better stay away from that. You know how O'Connor is about his family. He will tear you limb from limb if you so much as look at his little girl. If you want a little action, I can set you up with Alice. We all call her Good-Time Allie! She'll take care of your needs. Had her myself! Damn good stuff!"

"No, I don't want any used goods! I can get that from my ole lady! I want something new! Untouched! That way I can show her a whole new world!"

Laughing, Fred said, "Oh well, it'll be your ass!"

Slapping Jack on the back, he went back inside.

Watching all the activity across the street, Jack moseyed across and entered the store.

"I want some service!" he yelled, pounding on the counter.

Hearing the commotion, Katie headed toward the front.

Joseph stopped her before she got far. "I'll take care of this!"

"What the hell you think you're doing, scaring my customers!" Joseph lashed out at Jack.

"I want a bottle!"

"This is not a liquor store! Get the hell out!" Joseph took Jack by the arm and led him out the door. "If I ever see your face in my store ever again, I won't be as polite!"

Jack, stumbling and trying to walk, turned to face Joseph and said, "You son of a bitch! You can't tell me what I can and can't do!" Jack crossed back across the street to collect his car and drove off.

Jackie knew her dad had not been home much that week. When he was, he always went straight out back, sawing, hammering, working on some project until late at night.

Jackie followed him one evening, wondering what he was doing. She watched him carry wood down the steps to the cellar below. She got as close as she could without her father seeing her and hid behind a tree. Looking through the one and only window, she saw him building walls in the room where she used to play. Puzzled and wondering why, she quickly went back to the house before getting caught by her father.

Cleaning the house and doing the dishes, she wanted to make her daddy happy.

As her mama watched, Maddy realized her little girl was the only adult in the family.

Frowning as she pulled Jackie toward her, she said, "Honey, I am sorry, baby doll, that you have to do this. You should have friends to play with…and just be a little girl"

"Mommy, it's okay, I like doing this. Go back to bed. I'll be okay! Really!"

Hugging her tight, Maddy just walked into her bedroom and gently closed the door.

CHAPTER 2

Madeline

Madeline

Madeline did not come from a life such as this. She had wonderful parents who loved and adored her. Being an only child of George and Carolyn Moore, she had a wonderful life. They moved to Albuquerque when Madeline was in sixth grade. An accountant for a small business, her father had the opportunity for a better life. He had received an offer from a larger, well-established company to manage the whole accounting department. To take this new job, they had to move to Albuquerque, New Mexico. In a family discussion, they all agreed to take the chance. Madeline had to start all over and make new friends. At the age of twelve, girls already had a best friend;

and being new to the community, it was challenging. After six years, she had lots of friends and was the head of her class at school.

That was until she met Jack Hayes! She was so excited an older man was interested in her, a very handsome man. Not that Madeline wasn't pretty, she was, she just wasn't as interested in boys like her friends; her studies kept her busy. She did not know it was to be the beginning of hell! She soon found herself falling head over heels with him, which gave him the opportunity to lead her down the path of no return!

Her senior year she lost her virginity to the man she thought she loved and loved her. Wrong! Becoming pregnant at only seventeen, she was terrified! "What am I going to do?" she cried out many times to herself. She no longer had any close girlfriends, Jack made sure of that. She couldn't talk to her mother; they had forbidden her to see him.

Not knowing what else to do, she told Jack. He right away asked her to marry him. Feeling she had no other choice, Maddy said yes. Happy for their future together, both went to give her parents the good news. Their plans were not the news her parents wanted to hear.

"Pregnant? Getting married! How much do you even know about this Jack Hayes?" were just a few of the questions fired out by her parents.

"Mother, I love Jack, and he loves me. That is all I need to know about him. We want to be together, raising our baby."

"Well, that is not gonna happen!" shouted her father.

In tears, Madeline ran up to her room, slamming the door behind her. That gave Jack no other choice but to leave the house alone, slamming the door behind him. Their exciting news did not turn out the way he had hoped. Two days later they eloped.

Six hours later they arrived in Phoenix, Arizona. After saying their "I dos," they drove to the best hotel in town to make a reservation.

"Honey, give me your money, and I'll pay for our room. Only the best for my girl!" Jack assured his new bride.

"I don't have any money," Maddy replied.

"No cash! I thought you'd be smart enough to at least get some!" Jack degraded her.

"I didn't have time. You called late yesterday to meet you. I do have money in my bank account, and we can just withdraw as we need. Also my credit card," Maddy defended herself.

"Oh! Okay then. Let's get some now," he said, pulling up to a bank ATM. "Get $2,000."

Getting out of the car and walking up to ATM, she made the withdraw. Taking the money, Maddy climbed back into the car.

As he grabbed the bills out of her hand, she cried out, "Hey, that's mine!"

"No…it's mine! What's yours is mine now!" he said, laughing.

"Wait a minute!" she cried, trying to take the bills back from him. That was when the first slap came. Holding her cheek, she said, "You hit me! How dare you!"

"Yes, and I will again if you don't do as you are told," Jack said as he put the cash into his wallet. "Now let the honeymoon begin!"

Maddy, slumped against the passenger door, did not realize this was just the beginning!

Jack

Jack moved from town to town, finding odd jobs. Working just enough to get him by was the way he lived his life—day by day! Carpentry, being his line of work, made it easy for him to always get a job.

Jack lived his life like the life he was raised in, day by day! He did not know each day where his next meal was coming from. His mother left when he was only six years old, leaving Jack with only his father to raise him. When Leo went to work, he'd leave the six-year-old locked inside the house every day all by himself with only crackers to eat. Jack soon learned to crawl out a window, and from the local grocery, he learned to steal. He found the way to survive. When he turned twelve, life got better; he was able to go to work with his father each day.

At night, when Leo Hayes would come home with a woman, Jack would be given five dollars and told, "Find some other place to sleep." Night after night he had to sleep in their car, with only enough money to buy a sandwich. Every day since his mother left, he'd watch his ole man make beautiful things from the wood he brought home. When he turned sixteen, his father gave him a gift, a woman! Jack became a man that night. He learned from the best—drinking, women, and the skill of working with wood.

He worked every day with his father, and at night he worked the women. He learned fast that if the lady wouldn't do as he asked, she was quickly convinced.

When Jack turned eighteen, one night when he came home from a date, he found his father fast asleep on the sofa, or so he thought! Unable to wake him, he then saw the needle that was stuck in his arm. Quickly he threw some things in a bag. Jack was out the door and on his own. Town to town he did not stay in one place too long until he came to Albuquerque, New Mexico.

Coming to Albuquerque, he realized quickly how much he liked the town, especially when he met Madeline Moore, a red-haired, green-eyed beauty. He found her working as a cashier at the local grocery. Jack liked what he saw and kept going back every day to pick up small items so he could get to know the young lady. At her young age, she was perfect. The younger they were, the easier it was for him to control them. He followed her after work, learning where she lived and that she was a senior in high school. After seeing the house she lived in, the cars they drove, and how they well they dressed, he decided Madeline was the girl for him. She lived in a beautiful two-story house in town. It was obvious they had money, and he wanted some of it! As he charmed his way into her heart, he was finally able to persuade her to go to dinner with him.

Madeline knew Jack was older and that her parents would not approve, so she secretly met with him. She told her mom she was meeting a friend at the library to study; all the lies she began to tell so she could be with Jack after school, after work, whenever she could steal a few minutes, to make time to be with him. She loved how he made her feel and the kisses they shared. Jack was becoming her whole world. Cutting classes came next. Maddy lost her virginity in the back seat of his old Ford. Crying afterward, he held her tight, smiling; Jack knew he had her hooked. He wanted it all, a life like hers! If that had to include Madeline to get it...

Katie was the happiest working in the store. She liked being around people and helping them in all their needs. Going away to school in Santa Fe, she would be away from home and away from her friends. If school meant she could help even one person or family, it would be worth all she would be missing.

She put those thoughts aside when a customer approached her.

"Were you able to find all that you needed?" she asked him before ringing up the purchases.

Bagging the purchases, he went out the door.

Hearing the door reopen, she looked up to greet her next customer.

"Hi, Mr. Gordon, how can I help you? You going hunting or fishing?"

"Hey, Kaitlyn! I didn't know you were working. I can't get away this month for fishing, so I decided to go bear hunting in September. Me and the guys are going back to the Santa Fe National Park." He pulled a list out of his pocket. "This is what I need to start with…"

James Gordon lived twenty miles out of town with his wife, Teresa. In their late fifties, they had lived in the Albuquerque area for over thirty years. James had worked for the United States Postal Service since he was eighteen. Taking an early retirement, James became a true fisherman. He was known for taking long fishing trips at all the popular spots. He also loved to hunt—whatever the season—deer, elk, or bear. He was known for getting a trophy mule deer every year, and on occasion he would donate the prized mount for display in the store. A regular at the O'Connor store and good friend of her family, Katie left her station to help him in his shopping.

Katie worked for her father after school and on weekends, and she had to know all that was needed in the hunting and fishing business. Albuquerque was known for its many hot spots for fishing. The Navajo Dam, three hours north, provided good fishing. Many others surrounded the area. Hunting was also popular for those who enjoyed the thrill of the hunt. Bear and deer season were August to November. If you love deer-hunting, that season was between October and January. It was her job to know what every customer wanted or needed as supplies.

Jack Hayes was in town every day that week, watching Katie and learning her work schedule.

He would stay late, watching her comings and goings. Sitting on the bench outside the Laundromat, which was next door, he was able to see everything. Getting thrown out of the store and told never to come back by O'Connor, Jack, after making sure O'Connor was away, would enter the store and pretend to be shopping. Trying to be unnoticed, he would take a cart and go up and down aisles, looking at items close to the checkout stations. He'd pick up items, pretending to be interested, giving him the opportunity to watch Katie. He would not purchase anything, parking the cart to the side, then walk out quietly as he walked in, with his head down.

He dreamed of Kaitlyn O'Connor. He had a plan…a plan to make her his. It would make his life more enjoyable than what he had at that time. Smiling, his eyes closed, he was waiting for that perfect time to make his move.

Maddy knew something was going on. Jack was gone all day and would not show up at home until late. Then he'd work outside until dark. When he was in the house, he was always yelling and screaming at her and Jackie.

"Honey, what's wrong?" she'd ask.

Looking up from the table, he'd shout, "What's wrong! What's wrong! What isn't wrong! What little you cook isn't worth eating! You can't even clean yourself up! You don't even try to take care of me! Which I couldn't give a rat's ass! You were supposed to get me into your family's business. *But no!* What good are you to me now?"

"Honey, you know what happened when I approached them about that. After we ran off and got married, they wanted nothing more to do with me or their grandchild. They said I made my bed…" Reaching for his hand, she pleaded, "Jacky, baby, please let's talk."

"*No!*" he screamed as he slapped her hand away. "Don't touch me! You pathetic, old woman!" Jack then stormed out the door.

Maddy again started crying, knowing she was losing her husband. She knew, even how horrible her life was and how terrible he treated her, he was still her husband. There was no longer any love between them, and they hadn't slept in the same bed for years. He'd drink himself into a stupor and pass out in his chair every night. Like her parents said, she made her bed!

The house she and Jack lived in needed a lot of work. Ten years ago, when they moved there, Jack was so happy. It was almost like having the man she married back. He still had a temper, and if things did not go as he wanted, he took his frustrations out on her. He had big dreams of fixing up the place. Jack worked alongside Maddy, fixing broken things around the house. With his skills, he was able to fix the porch railings, the broken windows. He even built a porch swing for them all to sit and swing in the cool evenings. Maddy put in a little garden and was so excited when her vegetables began growing. Tomatoes, cucumbers, lettuce, potatoes, and corn filled the root cellar after the harvest. In the evenings as they swung, they shared their dreams. Jackie grew into a little girl. Then the loss of their second baby was when the drinking came back.

Jackie saw what went on between her parents and often ran to console her mother. Even at her young age, she knew all was not good between them.

"Mommy, it will be okay! I'm here! Don't cry!"

She hoped it was true.

CHAPTER 3

Married

Madeline

The newlyweds arrived back in Albuquerque two weeks later and drove straight to the house of Maddy's parents. George and Carolyn Moore were very upset that Madeline, against their approval, had run off and married *that* Jack Hayes. They had known by following her bank activity where she had gone and what was being spent. Seeing all the money being withdrawn proved them to be correct in their suspicions about him. They put a hold on their daughter's charge card to stop any further withdrawals. By doing this, they knew it would upset their daughter tremendously, but they had to teach her a lesson. She was now a married woman and on her own! They wanted to see Jack step up to the plate and start providing for his family.

"Mom, Dad, we're home!" Maddy called out, entering the house. Carolyn met her daughter in the entryway. "Mom please don't be mad! I love Jack. Please be happy for us."

"Honey, I don't know what to say! I am so disappointed!" Carolyn immediately told her daughter.

"Mom, please be happy for me! You're gonna be a grandma! Here comes Jack. Please be nice to him."

She opened the door and took her husband's hand as he entered the house.

"How can I be nice to someone who, against our approval, ran off with our daughter?"

Extending his hand, Jack just said, "Mrs. Moore."

Not accepting his shake, she only said, "Your father will home in an hour, and we'll talk then. Make yourselves at home." She then left them to themselves.

"Come up to my room. I need to get a few of my things, and I'll need your help," Maddy said, leading Jack toward her room.

As they walked up the staircase, he took in all the surroundings, the furnishings, the beautiful, polished floors, and all the paintings on the walls. At the top of the stairs was her bedroom. Maddy shut the door behind them. Jack immediately took Maddy into his arms and pushed her down onto the bed. He then then proceeded to unbutton her top.

"Stop! We haven't the time! We've got things to do. Besides, Mom…"

As she tried to resist, Jack stopped her with his kiss, "No, babe! You will never tell me *no*! What I want to do right now is take daddy's little girl right under his nose, under his own roof! You are mine! And you will *always* do as I command! You hear me!"

Maddy just looked at him. Immediately after getting married, Jack changed. It was his personality; he went from being a sweet, generous man to a hateful, mean person. Lying back on the bed, Jack once again took her. No pleasing her, just pleasuring himself. Maddy, with her eyes closed, bit down hard on her lip and caused it to bleed. This was not making love. It was just sex! No gentleness! Afterward Jack climbed off her and the bed and zipped up his pants. Maddy straightened her clothes and reapplied her lipstick. As she put a smile on her face, both went downstairs to greet her father, whom she had heard come home.

"Dad, how are you?" she asked, hugging him, "You remember Jack?"

George Moore greeted Jack with a brief handshake and said, "Let's all go into the study to talk." Leading the way, he took a seat in his favorite chair with Carolyn at his side. Jack and Madeline sat on the sofa.

George stood to address the couple, "Madeline, I won't say I'm happy about all this 'cause I'm not!"

"But Dad…"

"No!" he said, holding up his hand. "Hear me out first, then you can have your say. As I was starting to say, I am upset! No, furious, about what you two did! And you, young man, did you realize she is underage? She is only seventeen years old, and you are what… twenty-five? Isn't she a little young for you?"

"Wait just a minute, sir!" Jack said, jumping up to stop her father. "I will not let you talk to me this way. Yes, I know her age! Yes, I know I could get into trouble! But I fell in love with your daughter." Taking her hand into his, he gently kissed it.

"Trouble? We are talking jail time!"

"*Dad!* You wouldn't!" Maddy shouted out.

"Yes! I could, but I won't! A baby is involved now. I have a proposition, and let me finish before you lash out."

Jack sat back down beside Maddy on the sofa; they held hands and waited.

George again addressed the couple, "Here's what we do, annul the marriage!" Jack once again started to jump up, but George held up his hand. "No, hear me out… Annul the marriage, and Madeline stays here where we can take care of her. She has the baby, we put it up for adoption, and she can finish high school. Then go on to college to make something of herself."

"No! Not my baby!" Maddy screamed out.

"Okay, if you want to keep the baby, we could hire a nanny to help take care of it. Once you're back on your feet, Madeline, if you two feel the same way, your mother and I will give you a proper wedding. The wedding you have always dreamed about." George sat back down. "Okay, let's hear your thoughts. Two years college, Madeline, that's all I am asking for."

"Dad, we're already married. I will be eighteen in three months. Why can't we just go on as we are? I don't need a big, fancy wedding. All I want is Jack and our baby," Maddy insisted.

Jack saw things were not going the way he had hoped and spoke up, "Sir, I love your daughter and will work hard to make a good life for her and our baby. I will prove to you what kind of man I am."

"Well, that was my and your mother's terms. *I will not accept* what you have done! My hands are tied. If you don't agree to our terms, then I guess you both are on your own! No help from us!" George concluded, turning his back on them.

"Mom, Dad, you don't mean that. It's your grandchild!" Maddy cried out to her parents.

"Sorry, honey, I agree with your father. You heard our terms! It's that or nothing!"

"Is that why my charge card declined? You closed it!" Maddy spat at her.

"Yes, dear. You are a married woman now and on your own. Just kindly leave my house!" Carolyn spoke softly.

"At least let me get my things," Maddy said.

"No. I will send them to you," her mother replied.

Jack and Maddy left the only home she knew to start their new life.

Things only got worse. They found a small apartment in Los Lunas, some twenty-five miles away. Jack was able to find carpentry work, working long hours, which he did not like. His goal was to get a nice, cushy job with Maddy's dad. But no! Things did not work out the way he had hoped.

Maddy's marriage was turning out not what she had expected. She wanted her ever after, like her parents in the evenings, talking about their future! Their dreams! Holding each other close! No! Nothing even came close to that happiness. Jack was always coming home smelling of whiskey, wanting sex, then falling asleep immediately after. No care for her feelings at all. The fighting continued, and the beatings became more aggressive. Everything seemed to make him mad, and then he would strike out at her. Many times she had to cover her face heavily with makeup and wear sunglasses to hide the black eyes and bruised face. It was a miracle she had not lost the baby. They needed all the income they could get, so she worked all different shifts at the local diner in town, waitressing on her feet ten to twelve hours a day. She tried putting back money each week for doctor bills. Her cash tips and Jack's income paid the bills. Her paycheck, small that it was, was put back for the doctor and any emergency that always seemed to arise: car problems, dental. Jack had hit her one time so hard he knocked her to the floor, which caused her to break a tooth. That resulted in a huge dental bill.

Trouble always seemed to follow them. Jack would get into an occasional fight at a bar, which meant bail and court fees. The harder she tried, the more she fell behind. Maddy would cry at any moment due to her condition, and Jack, seeing this, of course, would get mad. He did not care or try to understand about her feelings and would just take some of the emergency fund and go out to drink, leaving

Maddy all alone. She was always having to find new places to hide the money. With all his anger issues, she learned to stay out of his way. It was like they had started living separate lives.

The only blessings were Maddy's bosses. The diner was jointly owned by Clara Johnson and Ruth Evans. The two sisters, after losing their spouses, went together and bought this diner. They took a liking to Maddy and treated her like a daughter.

Maddy was so afraid that when they found out she was pregnant she might be fired.

But no! When they did find out about her condition, they started treating her like a princess.

When she arrived for her shift in the early mornings, they made sure she had a big breakfast and a cold glass of milk waiting for her every day. She was given permission to take home any leftovers from the daily special, and this helped a lot in their budget. They became the family she no longer had.

As the months flew by, and Maddy's delivery grew close, the other waitresses and owners gave her a baby shower. It was her last day of work, before the birth of her child. Seeing all the beautifully wrapped gifts, Maddy realized what wonderful friends they had all become. She felt a sadness, knowing this was her last day, since she would be staying home with the baby. She loved being there. At the diner she was a different person, a stronger person, more outgoing and cheerful, greeting each customer with a smile. Back at her own home, she would revert back to that withdrawn person, afraid to face the world and her husband. Before leaving, the sisters told her that a job would always be available if she ever needed it. She lived down the street, within walking distance, and was told to not be a stranger and to stop in anytime with the baby for a fresh piece of pie.

Jack picked her up and barely helped her load the gifts into the car. She went home with a heavy heart. She was already worrying on how they were to survive. The free meals helped tremendously. Now she had to take more and more from the emergency fund to buy groceries. Jack was never in a good mood when he came home from work every evening.

Soup was about all they could afford, and he grew tired of that fast. He was sick of eating the same thing over and over.

"Where's my meat?" he would yell.

He also hated seeing Maddy, huge with child, and often called her a fat cow. Jack soon just started having his meals from the bottle.

Life was good in the Hayes family.

The day the baby came was yet another disappointment.

"A girl! Not a boy! Woman, can't you do anything right?" Jack screamed at her. "Where's my son? You were supposed to give me a son!"

Maddy was only able to see the doctor on occasion. Having no insurance, and money was so tight, an ultrasound telling them the gender of the child was not possible. The child, at the time of the birth, was going to be a surprise for them both.

"But Jack, she is so beautiful! She has your cute little nose! Come hold your daughter," Maddy pleaded with him then handed her to him as he came close to the hospital bed. "I want to name her Jacqueline, after her handsome daddy!

"Whatever!" he said, quickly handing the child back.

These days nothing made Jack happy. Taking the baby from him, she began rocking and singing softly to her, the same songs her mama sang to her when she was small.

"My precious little girl! My Jackie! Mommy loves you so much."

Life was quiet in the Hayes family for months. Little Jackie was learning to walk at eight months old, and Maddy excitedly watched her daughter's attempts and falls. Not letting the falls scare her, Jackie would grab onto a table, pull herself up, and try again. Maddy would run over, snatch her little girl up, and hug her dearly. Jack wanted nothing to do with his daughter. On occasion, in the middle of the day when Jack wanted sex, Maddy would have to put her daughter in her play pen and abide by her husband's wishes. She learned early never to say *no* to him.

Jack was caught drinking on the job and was fired immediately. With Maddy still not working, times got very rough. The emergency fund got smaller and smaller: baby needs, groceries, and more than often, Jack stealing from it to get his regular bottle.

Maddy had always been very good at budgeting, but now there were no longer incomes to budget!

Taking a part-time job back at the diner helped a little. With Jack offering no help with the baby, Maddy was forced to bring her with her. When Jackie was three months old, she left her in Jack's care to run an errand. Upon returning, she found Jack fast asleep on the couch and the baby crying her little heart out on the floor. Hitting him with all her might, she screamed, "How could you? One afternoon! Just one afternoon is all I asked for me to do the shopping!" That was the first and last time she left her with Jack.

The owners, seeing how Maddy was struggling, just shook their heads. They knew what a useless man she was married to. They also heard rumors about his infidelity. It was a wonder Maddy had not heard anything, or if she did, she did not show it. They all tried many times to make her come to her senses and leave him. Even many of her regular customers pleaded with her to let them help. But no, Maddy would not leave Jack. She was determined to make her marriage work even though she was very much afraid of him.

One afternoon Jack came storming through the door of the house, shouting, "Start packing! We're moving!"

Maddy closed the door of the baby's room gently.

"The baby is sleeping," she shushed at him.

"Pack! We are moving! A friend is letting me have a small piece of land. Five acres just outside the park of the Sandia Mountains some eleven miles from Edgewood."

"Out of town? What if we need a doctor? I like living here in Los Lunas."

"We will be fine!" he said, taking Maddy's hands. "This is my chance! Our chance! Baby, we need this! A new life!" Jack said, begging.

Maddy had never seen Jack this excited, not in a long time.

"Okay! Let's do it! Start all over!"

Heading into the kitchen, she began taking dishes out of the cabinets and stacking them on the table. Three days later the Hayes headed out. Telling all her friends goodbye was one of the hardest things Maddy had to do. Again! Being thrown out of her own home was not as hard as this; Maddy had come to love everyone there. But she had to do it to save her marriage.

Every day Jack watched Katie working at the store. He dreamed of how it would feel having her beneath him, with her doing what he demanded and what he wanted to do to her. Thinking of her he felt an arousal, a first in a long time. Time was running out; he had only had two days remaining to get what he wanted. And what he wanted was Kaitlyn O'Connor! He heard that Friday was to be her last day of work, and he knew he had to make his move *quick!*

Jack made it at home that night at a decent time, and he was able to finish his project. He was ready! He then called for his daughter.

"Honey, I need you to come into town with me tomorrow morning and help your daddy. This is strictly just between us. Your mommy is to know nothing! It's kind a like a surprise for her!" Taking her cheeks in his rough hands and squeezing them. "Understand!"

Nodding, "Yes, Daddy. I like surprises! Especially for mommy," she replied happily.

Early the next morning, as Jack and his daughter prepared to leave for town, Maddy confronted him, "Why are you taking Jackie with you this morning? You've never had her go with you before! Why now?"

Pushing her aside, he said, "I need her help! Get your ass back in there"—pointing toward the house—"Tonight you will fix a good meal 'cause we are having company."

"Mommy, it's a surprise! Please let me go," Jackie begged of her mother.

Hearing the excitement in her daughter's words, she said, "Okay, sweetheart, just mind your manners," giving her a quick kiss.

In town Jack took Jackie into the alley behind the O'Connor Fish and Game building.

"Honey, this is what I want you to do…"

There was an alley that ran between the O'Connor's store and the laundry mat. Trash bins were on both sides behind each building. The areas surrounding the bins were covered with trash from the garbage collectors being so sloppy in their routes, dropping any excess to the ground and leaving litter all over. The sheriff was always on both businesses, urging them to clean up the area. They, in turn, called the trash collectors complaining of the problem. It was an ongoing matter. The small alley ran on to join with another street, giving a garbage truck plenty of room to turn around.

"But why, Daddy?" Jackie asked her father.

"Because I said so!" Jack answered.

"I don't know if I can pretend to cry!" she informed him.

Slapping her across the face, he said, "Now you can! Go!"

He went to hide behind the trash bins, eagerly waiting for his plan to come to life.

Running through the front doors, "Lady! Lady! Please help me!" Jackie begged.

Dropping what she was doing, Katie ran toward the crying girl.

Drawing her close, she said, "Honey! What's wrong?" holding her tight.

Jackie was sobbing, "My puppy! My puppy! Please help me, she is hurt!" Taking Katie's hand, Jackie led the way into the back alley where her father was impatiently waiting.

Katie looked all around for a little puppy.

"Where is it?"

Crying harder, Jackie said, "I'm sorry! I am so sorry! Daddy made me do it!"

Looking back at the girl, "What!" she asked, totally confused.

That was the last thing Katie heard. The next thing she saw was *darkness*!

CHAPTER 4

Taken

Katie woke to find herself in a dark room…not hers! With only a small amount of light that was coming through a small window, she was unable to see much. Trying to figure out where she was, she sat up on the bed and felt something pull against her ankle. It was a chain!

Feeling something dangle on her head, she found what she thought to be a pull chain. As she pulled hard, it turned on a light, allowing her to see her surroundings. To her horror, brick walls covered in cobwebs, a dirt floor, and the small very dirty window. She was not able to look out; it was just above her head. She found a chair and dragged it under the window. As she climbed upon it, she was able to look out, seeing nothing but dirt. "Am I underground?" Katie said to herself. Taking another look, she could barely see the top of the ground. "Where am I?" she asked herself. Stepping down off the chair, she sat back down on the old cot and examined the chain. Katie noticed it was attached to a pole in the center of the room.

"Hello! Hello! Is anyone out there?" she called out.

Back in town, Joseph called home, "Margaret, by any chance, is Katie there?"

"No, dear! I thought she was at the store working with you. Why?" his wife answered.

"She's not here! She's nowhere to be found!"

"What do you mean, can't be found! She left with you this morning."

Joseph ordered his wife, "Get on the phone and call all her friends. Maybe something came up, and one of them needed her help, and she left to meet them.

"She wouldn't just leave without telling someone. Did you ask the others? Maybe she did let someone know about having to step out for a few minutes," Margaret insisted. She just hung up the phone with her husband and started to make her calls.

Kaitlyn

Kaitlyn, known as Katie, the daughter of Joseph and Margaret O'Connor, grew up to be the darling of Albuquerque, New Mexico. As she grew up, she was always at the store, either sitting on her grandpa's lap or getting in everyone's way. She knew everybody in town and treated them all like family. Everyone saw her grow from a blond-haired, blue-eyed little girl in pigtails to a beautiful young lady. Margaret, unable to have additional children, was happy just having Katie.

Margaret met Joseph at the grocery in Edgewood, where Margaret taught school. It was love at first sight. They started dating and would get together several times a week. Although they were older, when they were together, they felt like teenagers again. Both in their thirties, they quickly realized they were meant for each other. Joseph took Margaret to his home to meet to his parents. That same day he proposed. His parents knew right away that Margaret was the perfect match for their son. Margaret had lost her parents years before and had no other relative. She was welcomed with open arms into her new family. Margaret, with her soon-to-be mother-in-law's help, organized her wedding. Both Joseph and Margaret had their own money, so no financial help from his parents were needed. Margaret gave up her teaching job in Edgewood and moved to Albuquerque. She moved in with Joseph's family until their wedding day.

Margaret wanted a simple wedding, with only close friends invited. Joseph's best friend, Jim Gordon, was his best man. Jim's wife, Teresa, stood beside Margaret. On her wedding night, Margaret became pregnant. She was so excited. She never dreamed she would have her own child. All the children in her class was her family. She became a stay-at-home mom while Joseph went to work with his father.

Being an only child, you could not call Katie spoiled. She was known for helping others in all their needs. At lunch she would trade her lunch to another for a bruised apple or overripe banana to give that friend something better to eat, letting herself go hungry. Many times, in the cool evenings, Katie would come home from playing outside without her sweater. saying she lost it. Her mother, knowing what really happened, would just shake her head and laugh.

For graduation, Katie was given the surprise of a seven-day cruise with two of her friends before entering college. Libby and Lisa joined her on that wonderful trip visiting New Orleans, Cozumel, and Yucatan. All three had a wonderful time hanging out on the beautiful beaches.

In New Orleans Katie saw a different type of people, adults begging for money. They even had their own small children on the side of streets, entertaining the crowd for handouts, in dirty clothes and barefoot. She wondered, "Is this the life some have? Begging for food?"

Seeing all the hurt in the world helped her decide what to do with her own life, to help those in need: feed the hungry, clothe the poor, or even help the abused. Her mother totally agreed with her decision. Kaitlyn O'Connor was meant to help the needy. Her boyfriend, Charlie Watts, tried to understand, but he wanted to get married and start a family. Katie kept telling him she was not ready. She still had not given in to his urges to finalize their love for each other. She wanted the life she was meant to have first before settling down to her final chapter.

After it seemed like hours, Katie, sitting on the cot, finally heard a noise. Pushing herself back far as possible on the bed, she waited.

Jack unlocked the door and said, "Hello, darling! I see you're finally awake!"

Adjusting her eyes as glared at the man before her.

"*I know you!*" She pointed her finger at him. "You were in the store first of the week, causing all kinds of trouble. What am I doing here? And what is this?" she asked, shaking the chain at him.

"It will be removed once I know you can be trusted," Jack informed her.

"What do you mean, trusted? I have to go home!" Katie ordered.

"You will…in due time! When I have my fill of you!"

"What you mean? I want to go home now! My mom and dad will be sick with worry," she cried out.

Jack answered, "Like I said, all in good time!"

Looking around the room, she saw a sink and small mirror in a back corner, but no toilet!

"Where's the toilet?" She thought maybe it was in another room. "I have to use the toilet."

"See that white bucket?" he said, pointing in the corner. "Have at it!"

"You've got to be kidding!"

"Nope! It's all yours!" Jack was laughing. Remembering the chain on her ankle, he said, "I will give you a chance and take that off"—he pointed toward the shackle—"so you can go to the bath-room. Just don't try anything!"

With it removed, Katie rushed over to the sink and ran water into her hands to wash. Seeing herself in the mirror, she had a dirty face with mascara running down it. Her long blond hair was tangled and uncombed. Humiliated, she went ahead and took care of her business in front of her captor. After finishing, she rose and slowly walked toward her bed. Taking a chance, she bolted toward the door.

Jack realized what was happening, grabbed her by the hair, and slammed her to the ground. He placed his knee across her chest and held her arms down all while Katie kicked and screamed at him.

"Stop it! Shut the fuck up!" Jack shouted, punching her in the face, causing blood to cover her face.

"You pull that stunt again…try to escape…I will kill you! We can do this the easy way, or we can do it the hard way! It's up to you."

"Why are you doing this? What have I done to you?" Katie asked hysterically.

Pulling her up from the hard ground, he threw her upon the bed. Sitting beside her, he took her leg and refastened the shackle around her ankle.

"I guess I have my answer about trust."

As he ran his fingers up her leg and stopped at her thigh, Katie pushed his hand away.

Laughing, Jack rose to leave and said, "You can yell and scream as loud as you want. No one can hear you. So you might as well save your breath. I'll be right back to bring you something to eat."

Jack shut the door. Hearing it being locked, Katie wiped the blood from her nose, curled up on the bed, and cried.

Maddy met Jack at the door as he entered the house and asked, "What's going on?"

Pushing her aside he said, "Woman, it's nothing you need to know about."

As Jack ate his dinner, he ordered his wife to fix a plate of food.

"Why another plate?"

"Like I said, we have company."

Jack took the second plate and headed out the door. Maddy watched her husband walk toward the back of the yard. Jackie saw her mother peeking out the window.

"Mommy, I did something very bad!"

"Honey, what could you have done that was so bad? Not you, baby!" her mommy assured her.

"Yes, Mommy, I helped daddy get a girl and bring her here."

Pulling her close, Maddy said, "What! What girl?"

"That girl whose daddy owns the fishing store. The one who's always nice to me!" Jackie started to cry.

"Kaitlyn! Kaitlyn O'Connor! She's here?"

"Yes, Mommy!"

"Oh dear! What's he planning?"

"I don't know, Mommy. Daddy made me get her outside to the back of the store. He hit her, carried her to his car, and brought her here. He drove the car around back to the cellar and carried her inside. He made me stay outside."

The root cellar was at the far end of the yard, dug out of the mountainside. Double doors on a mound of dirt led the way down to the room underground, the same room Jack had been working on for weeks. Through the double doors and at the bottom of the steps was another door, which Jack installed. In this room was where he kept Kaitlyn O'Connor, far enough away where no screams could be heard. If you didn't know the cellar was there, you would never find it. All that was kept in the cellar were vegetables and canned goods. They were kept better in the cooler temperature.

"Daddy told me it was a surprise for you to get me to go into town with him. If I've known this was gonna happen, I wouldn't gone. But Mommy, I was so excited getting a surprise for you."

Jackie cried harder. Maddy pulled her daughter close.

"Oh dear! What is he planning?" she asked herself.

Jack unlocked the door and entered the cellar.

"Here, I brought you a little something to eat. It's not much, but it will do for now," said Jack, setting the plate on the bed beside her.

Katie picked up the plate and threw it, food flying in all directions.

"I want to go home!"

"Girlie! Why'd you do that?"

"Please let me go home. I won't say anything," she pleaded.

"Not till I am done with you!" Jack answered in an angry voice.

"What do you want with me?" she asked.

"Soon!" he answered as he picked up the pieces of the plate and silverware, "I guess you'll have to learn to eat when given to you! You can just do without tonight."

He shut the door behind him. Katie jumped up.

"*No! Wait!* Please, I'm sorry. Don't leave me!" she cried out.

CHAPTER 5

Missing

Hearing nothing from Katie all day, Joseph made a call to the Albuquerque sheriff's department. After several minutes of talking with Sheriff Dave Thomas, Joseph was informed he had to wait forty-eight hours before declaring Kaitlyn O'Connor a missing person.

"Goddammit, Dave! You know she wouldn't just leave without telling anyone in the store. Something is wrong!"

"Joseph, I'm sorry! Tell you what, I will send out one of my men to look around town and see what they might find. Are you sure she didn't just take off with Charlie? I heard she was dating him. A few years now?"

"No! She would have told someone something…Libby! She and Charlie broke up weeks ago. Margaret called and left a message at his folk's house. No one is at home."

"Well, see! Think about it! Charlie missing! Katie missing!" the sheriff answered.

"*No!* I will not accept that! Something is wrong! I guess I'll have to do your job by going out myself to look! *You* will hear from me early Sunday morning in exactly forty-eight hours!" Joseph slammed the phone down.

After picking up Margaret at the house, they drove all over town, first stopping at Libby's and Lisa's houses and finding they had no additional information. Both girls also went out, searching for Katie. Stopping at the Watts house a few miles out of town, Joseph and Margaret still found no one at home. Driving around all that Friday night and finding nothing about their daughter's whereabouts, Joseph began to think that the sheriff might be right. Katie might be with Charlie. He hoped she was. But it still was not like his daughter to take off without telling someone of her plans.

They arrived back at their house around 3:00 a.m.; both hoped to find Katie safe in her bed fast asleep. Rushing through the front door, they found the house dark, and no Katie.

After a quick nap, they drove back to town that Saturday afternoon. Joseph stopped first at his store to update his staff that he'd be gone the whole day. Fully satisfied that his manager could handle any problems that should arise, they picked up both Libby and Lisa and headed out again to visit all their stomping grounds. Their first stop was Charlie Watt's house.

Still finding no one at home, Joseph again questioned Libby, "You sure Katie is not with Charlie?"

"I am positive, Mr. O'Connor! Katie would have told me if she and Charlie were back together. She wanted to go away to school!"

She and Lisa were just as afraid of Katie's whereabouts as the others.

Driving around all day and late into the night to find no one knew where Katie was, the O'Connors finally gave up late in the evening and dropped the girls off at each their homes before heading to their own.

Early Sunday morning Joseph called the sheriff at his home. Knowing it to be Joseph, the sheriff answered with the question, "Katie's home safe in her own bed, right?"

"No, Dave, she is not! We were out until late Friday and Saturday night! We went out to see all her friends! Their hangouts! Libby and Lisa also drove around with us. Charlie Watts is still not home!"

"See…Think about it…"

"No! Katie would not do anything without saying anything! Libby even said Katie has not talked to him in weeks. Sheriff, can we do something now?" Joseph shouted out.

"Okay! Meet me at the office in fifteen minutes."

The O'Connors were already waiting at the department when he drove up. After grabbing a cup of coffee, he led them to his office. Grabbing a pen and paper, he started taking notes.

"Fill me in. how did the week go, did anything unusual happen?" he asked.

"Everything was normal. Well, except at the beginning of the week, Monday, I think. Jack Hayes came in drunk as a skunk! Causing a scene, I had to show him the door."

"Yeah, he's harmless! Drinks a little too much. I have to run him and that loser friend of his, Fred Gates, to jail every now and then for excessive drinking. I feel sorry for his family though. They're just barely surviving out at their place. I know Madeline is living a life she was not accustomed to. She came from a better lifestyle than that. I heard she was to be valedictorian of her class before she skipped out. She had a good head for numbers like her daddy and was going to school for accounting. I heard she already had a job waiting for her alongside him. That was…before she got mixed up with Jack Hayes.

Her folks just packed up and moved when she married him. They were so ashamed!"

"Yes, I knew George. Ten—eleven years ago, they just up and moved suddenly without a goodbye to anyone. I forgot all about that until you mentioned it just now. I thought I heard something about their girl. Katie was only seven at the time," Joseph added to the conversation.

"Yeah, it was a real mess then, so sad! I'll go out and pay Jack a visit in the morning and check up on Madeline. Now, when did you notice she was gone?" Dave asked once again, taking notes.

"It was after lunch. I heard a customer calling for help. Katie was supposed to be up front, working the register. That was when I noticed her gone," Joseph concluded.

"Let me grab a deputy, and let's head down to the store to look around."

Back at the store, Margaret found Katie's cell phone behind the counter.

"Katie wouldn't have left without her phone. That phone is in her hand 24-7!" Margaret informed the officer.

The sheriff took the phone and thumbed through the texts and calls to see who the last person she talked with. The last text showed the previous night with Libby. He redialed the last number, and Libby Jackson answered, saying they had talked the night before. The cell phone was of no help to them.

"I want to go around back and look around."

The sheriff started out the door but was met by his deputy in the doorway.

"I went ahead and started looking around back and found this on the ground among the litter," he said as he handed over a gold bracelet.

Margaret pushed past the men, saying, "That's Katie's! We gave that to her for graduation."

"Maybe it broke free when she was taking out the trash?" asked the sheriff.

"No! Look! The trash has not been dumped for two, three days!" Joseph pointed out the overflowing baskets. "Besides, our janitor takes care of that. Before I left Friday, I told everyone to not touch anything in the front area until we hear anything from Katie," Joseph informed them. "We also have security cameras pointed toward the front."

"Get me the video of that whole week. You have a camera outside too?" the sheriff again asked.

"Yes, we do," Joseph answered.

"What about out back?"

"Sorry, nothing in the back."

"Damn, that would have been too easy being able to see what happened back there. Wherever you have cameras, I want them all. Surely, one picked up something we can use."

"I hate to say this, but with Katie disappearing and the broken bracelet on the ground, it could mean something! Something I'm afraid of!" the sheriff told the others of his thoughts.

"What you mean, Dave?" Joseph asked.

"I'm not looking in that direction yet before I have a talk with the Watts boy. You sure you've not noticed anything strange? A person hanging around out of ordinary, watching everything and everybody!"

"*No!*" Margaret cried out, realizing what they were talking about.

Before heading back to his office, the sheriff pulled the deputy to the side and said, "Bring Libby Jackson and Lisa Koons into the office. I think they're Katie's good friends. Most of all, get me Charlie Watts!"

"Yes, sir!"

Later that afternoon the girls and their parents were waiting in the lobby at the department. All wanted to do their best to help. Dave noticed the Watts boy's absence, and the deputy informed him that there still was no one at home. With no further help from the girls, they were excused, leaving the sheriff to wait for the return of his possible suspect. He remembered Joseph was to bring him the film of that week's activity later that day.

Late that afternoon, Joseph O'Connor showed up at the precinct, full of anger.

"The goddamn cameras were down the whole week!" he blasted out. "One of the stockers *forgot* to reload the camera! All week! Of all the *luck*! It would have shown us what had happened that Friday. I fired his ass right then and there! You might as well say he might have just killed my little girl!"

"That really would have helped! Damn it!" The sheriff patted Joseph on the back. "Go home to Margaret, and let me do my job. I'll be in touch."

Monday morning Sheriff Thomas made the drive out to the Hayes place. As he drove down the lane toward the house, he took in all the surroundings. The house, the shape it was in, could be made into something to be proud of. The grounds were breathtaking with the Sandia Mountains in the background. Although desert was all around, it still was a beautiful site. There was a garden on one side of the house, which looked like it had been unattended to for years. The sheriff, shaking his head, proceeded on to the porch and knocked.

Madeline, opening the door, came face to face with the sheriff.

"Hello, Sheriff, what can I do for you?"

"Is Jack here? I need to speak with him."

"He's out back. Please come in." Maddy stepped aside to allow him to enter. "Have a seat, and I'll get him for you," she said, knowing exactly where he was but unsure how she was going to do it.

"No, that's okay. Don't bother him right this moment. I can wait. That will give us time to visit, if you don't mind?" He noticed Jackie peering around the doorway of her room. "Hello, young lady, you're growing up so fast!"

Jackie, not knowing how to answer the question, just ran to her mother's side.

"Jackie, you remember Sheriff Thomas. I know it's been a long time since we've been in town. School, the hot weather, we just stay here in the house."

The sheriff come straight to the point, "Madeline, do you need anything? You know you don't have to live like this! I can help! The town will help!"

Just as she started to answer, Jack walked through the door.

"I saw your car outside. What do I owe the pleasure for this visit?"

"Jack, I have a few questions for you about a visit you made in town few weeks ago. At the O'Connor store!"

Jackie buried her face in her mother's apron.

Jack, hearing this, broke out into a cold sweat and said, "Come on, let's step outside so we can talk in private."

"Oh, you don't want your wife to know how much you drink? Don't you think she already knows? About your little problem!" the sheriff shot at him.

"What the hell are you talking about?" Jack quickly asked.

"Last Monday the disturbance you caused in the store when you were totally wasted," the sheriff said, answering Jack's question.

Jack calmed himself, realizing he was safe. The sheriff was there on a totally different matter.

"Sheriff, really, that was last week, and you are here now? You would do anything to put me in jail! Tell you what… I will go in and personally tell Mr. O'Connor how sorry I am! Will that satisfy you? *Now kindly get your ass off my property!*"

"What you need to do is take better care of your family! Clean up this place. Look at it! The weeds need to be pulled around the house, fix these porch steps. You ever think about painting? I know you have the ability to do it, just not the want to!"

That was the sheriff's last warning to Jack before getting into his car and driving back to town.

It took all week to locate Charlie Watts, giving the sheriff hope that Katie just ran off with him. One of the deputy's assignments was to make it his first stop, at the Watts' residence, to look for Charlie. That Monday morning he found Charlie at home.

"Charlie, I have orders to bring you in for questioning."

"What kind of questions?" he asked the deputy, puzzled.

"You're to come with me now, and you will soon find out," the deputy replied as he escorted the young man to his car.

"Have a seat, Charlie," he said, motioning to a chair. "Where you been all week, and when was the last time you saw Kaitlyn?" he quickly asked.

Charlie slumped down in the chair.

"I took a few days off, me, the family, and a few of my buddies. We went fishing. I've not seen or talked with Katie in weeks. You see, she and I aren't exactly on speaking terms these days. Ever since she come home from her cruise, she changed. I wanted to get married, and she didn't! End of discussion!" Charlie answered.

"Where were you last Friday the fourteenth?"

"I was working out on Wilbur Road at the Phillips' place. We were helping him install a new septic system. Why?" Charlie was getting irritated from all the questions.

"Kaitlyn O'Connor is missing!" the sheriff informed him.

"Missing?" Charlie jumped to his feet. "*What the hell!* You think I have something to do with that? I love her!"

"Yes, but she didn't want to marry you! How did that make you feel Charlie? *Mad?*" the sheriff fired back at him.

"Now, wait just a minute. I want only the best for Katie! Sure, I was mad, and we had a huge argument, but I wouldn't hurt her for the world. Even though we're not together, I still love her. Are we through here?"

"Yes, just don't disappear again!"

Charlie was out the door so fast he didn't hear the sheriff's final words.

He took off running down the street toward the sporting-goods store. He had to get answers. Charlie rushed through the doors of the store and immediately spotted Katie's dad.

Stopping at his side, he blurted out, "Mr. O'Connor, please, have you found Katie? I just heard. You know I have nothing to do with her being missing. I love her!"

Pulling Charlie away from the main aisle, Joseph asked, "Son, where have you been? The whole town has been looking for you and Katie! Is she with you?"

His hopes ran high, thinking Katie would walk into the store behind Charlie.

"No, sir! I was away fishing with the family. Joey, Randall, and Robbie tagged along. You know them."

"Yes, I know them. Did Dave get ahold of you?" Joseph asked.

"Yes, he just told me. I swear to God I have nothing to do with this. She just wasn't ready to settle down. I understand that now! Not that I'm still upset about it. Katie is cool! She wouldn't have done anything crazy, like running off!" Charlie answered.

"I know, son! And that is why I am so afraid!" Joseph agreed.

The next morning, as Jack took breakfast to his captive, he had a spring in his step.

"I did it! *Goddamn*, I did it!" he said to himself as he unlocked the door. "Good morning, my lovely! You hungry for breakfast? You better eat today 'cause I don't like wasting food like you did yesterday," he said as he handed the plate to her.

This time Katie took the plate of food and began eating hungrily. She had not eaten since yesterday at breakfast.

"See, it ain't so bad! Once you learn to follow the rules, we can be a big happy family." Jack told her as she ate.

"I'll behave, I promise!" Katie agreed, but her mind was racing, still thinking of a way to escape.

"Now, see how easy this is, us talking?" Jack asked, grinning.

After she finished her meal, he took the plate and eating utensils back up to the house.

In the kitchen he found a bottle and took a big swig, not caring how early it was. Draining it before setting it on the table, Jack decided.

"I've waited long enough. Time to make her mine!"

Watching the door open, Katie realized her captor was back already. Her ceiling light was off, making the room dark except for what little light was coming through the window. She could hear him come closer to the bed. Shivering, she curled up tight as she could, praying. Placing a knee on the bed, Jack pulled the blanket off and dragged her toward him, roughly tearing open her blouse, making the buttons fly in every direction. She began kicking and screaming at him, trying to get away, but his body held her down. Yanking down her shorts, he made his demands. Loosening his belt and unzipping his pants, he lowered himself upon her while holding her arms together above her heard. His huge body crushed hers as he guided himself into her warm spot. He didn't bother to remove her panties, just shoved them to the side.

Still kicking and screaming at him, he entered her with great force, plunging into her, which made her scream even more while he just laughed.

"I knew you'd be untouched!" After, he ran his fingers down her thigh and said, "It was better than I expected!" Pulling up his pants, he left the dirty room, locking the door behind him.

Grabbing the blanket off the floor, Katie covered herself and sobbed. Her *hell* had just gotten worse!

CHAPTER 6

The Abuse

Life in the O'Connor house just stopped.

Ten days, and still no word. Margaret cried every day, sitting on Katie's bed, holding onto her graduation picture.

Joseph went to work, but only to go through the motions. He would just sit behind his desk and stare at the wall, willing the phone to ring, with Katie saying she was on her way home. It was a good thing he had a great staff to run the business. It all meant nothing to him these days. He would give it all away just to have his daughter back home, safe.

Jumping up from his chair, Joseph headed for the sheriff's office. When he got there, he ran in, pointing toward Dave's office.

"Is he in?" he asked the receptionist at the front desk.

She nodded her response and told him to go on back.

Entering the room, he blurted out, "Dave, have you heard..." before seeing him on the phone, stopped question.

The sheriff waved him in.

"Yes, sir, I understand! You say you've got men on their way? Great, thanks for your help," Dave said, replacing the phone on its stand. "Yes, Joseph, have a seat. I was just on the phone with the state police. They're sending men out to help us, with this being a possible kidnapping. They should be here late tomorrow."

"Have you found out anything? This waiting is killing us! I can't concentrate at work, just praying that the phone will ring. Margaret isn't sleeping. She just sits in Katie's room, looking at her picture. Why is this happening? You know Katie wouldn't just leave without telling someone of her plans," Joseph pleaded.

Dave went around to the front of his desk and sat on a corner.

"I know Joseph. We have help coming. I did go out to the Hayes place and talked with him. I didn't get anything out of him, and nothing seemed amiss. All he cares about is where his next bottle is coming from."

Jackie was getting quieter at home and keeping to herself more and more. She still went to school but complained often of a belly-ache or headache and begged to stay home. At recess Jackie would either stay inside reading a book or, if outside, she would swing on the swing sets by herself. Having nothing to do with any other boy or girl, she had become very withdrawn.

One evening, while sitting at the dining-room table, coloring, and her mother cooking, her daddy came in. Jackie jumped up and ran to her mother's side, almost knocking her down.

"Honey, you almost burned yourself," Maddy said, removing the pan of fried chicken off the burner and setting it to the side. As she turned around, she saw that her husband had come in. "Supper is almost ready. Go wash up." Maddy was taking more initiative to cook those days.

"I'll take my plate and eat with my guest tonight and from now on," Jack informed her.

"Jack, we need to talk about what's going on. Jackie told me what she did," Maddy said, letting him know what she had learned from their daughter.

He gave his daughter a stern look.

"I told you to keep your mouth shut!" Jack reminded her. Jackie held tighter onto her mother. "It doesn't matter anymore. I got the job done!"

"What are you thinking, bringing that girl *here*?" Maddy cried with fear in her words.

"You," he shouted, pointing his finger at his wife, "need to take care of your little girl and mind your own business! This is my house, and you will do as you are told!" Jack snarled, slapping her against the head.

At that moment Maddy realized her husband had lost his mind.

Taking the plates from Maddy, Jack headed toward the cellar. Katie saw the plates of food in his hands as he entered the room. Sitting together on the bed, they both ate.

"All the time I'll be spending here we need to get a bigger and softer bed and maybe a table and chairs for our little love nest." Katie didn't reply. Just as they finished eating, he announced, "Now time for dessert! I want the light on so I can see your body as I make love to my girl."

Removing the plates, he pushed her backward onto the bed and proceeded to undress her. Her top, ripped and torn, just barely covered her breasts. After he tore the remaining off, he began kissing her breasts. She kicked at her abuser, but he pinned her down on the thin mattress and straddled her. He roughly kneaded her breasts with his hands.

"I knew you had big titties!"

Biting them hard and leaving whelps all over them made Katie cry out in pain. Laying upon her, she could feel his hardness against her. She continued to scream, knowing it was useless to think anyone could help her, but she did it anyway. No one knew where she was, including herself! This time he removed her panties and threw them to the ground. She closed her eyes and bit down on her lip, causing it to bleed as Jack abused her body over and over.

"Gosh, dang! It gets better and better!" Rolling off her, he sat up on the side of the bed while he gathered her into his arms. "I'll be back later," he said, giving her a quick and sloppy kiss.

He then exited the room, locking it behind him.

Grabbing her blouse, Katie tried to cover herself. With the blouse torn to shreds, she found it impossible to close it over her breasts. Even as hot as it was, she took the blanket and wrapped it around her shoulders, trying to hide the bruises that were all over her body.

Jack was whistling as he walked up to the house. Damn, he was in a great mood. Good loving can do that to a man.

"Maddy, I'm going into town. I need to find work. It takes money to keep you all provided in the finest!" Turning her around to face him, he said, "Now *you* stay away from that cellar, you hear me! If I see anything wrong, I swear I will beat you senseless. Understand!"

"Yes, Jack!" Maddy said, agreeing as she cringed away from her husband.

CHAPTER 7

Press Conference

The state police showed up on day eleven. Sheriff Thomas was anxiously waiting.

Shaking hands, he asked, "What do we do next? We've not had a missing person at least since before I took office nearly ten years ago."

The trooper, after introducing himself as Lieutenant Reynolds, asked, "How do you know this is a missing person, or what you mentioned on the phone, a possible kidnapping? Was there a note, and did anyone see or hear anything?"

"No, nothing! That's what's so puzzling! I have known this girl all her life. A good kid! My first thoughts were, she ran off with her boyfriend, but after talking with him, I realized he knows nothing. He's just as worried about her as her family. Something *has* happened to her! We found her phone and was told by her mother she had it on her at all time. We looked at her last texts and calls and came up with nothing. Her last text and phone calls were from the previous night. We also have it in our presence in case anyone tries to reach her or might even know where she is. All we found was her bracelet out back by the trash cans. We've not said anything to the reporters yet until we had a chance to talk."

"That's good! Just fill me in on what you have done so far," the trooper stated. After looking over the notes, he said, "You've made a good start. We'll check out the surrounding businesses and talk with all the local homeowners close by again. Just in case someone happened to remember anything else. Any little thing they might have forgotten could really become a key point for us. Let's meet back eight o'clock in the morning."

The lieutenant shook Dave's hand then proceeded to give out orders to his men. Dave headed out to the O'Connors to update them of the state police's arrival.

Joseph could not understand why the sheriff had not posted anything in the papers or on the local news. The sheriff explained to him that he wanted to keep all the details quiet until the state police arrived. The businesses and townsfolks also were wondering about all the questions, and he just told them they would know soon. He wanted to make sure he was handling things properly before it hit the news.

Finally, with the state police's approval, the sheriff set up a press conference, letting the town know of the occurrence and to ask for any additional help. The sheriff and his men placed all through the town and other surrounding areas bulletins that stated the time and day on that late July that it was to be held.

On the steps in front of the courthouse, all news stations and newspaper reporters from the surrounding areas gathered in front, ready to hear the news. Margaret and Joseph O'Connor were ready to do their part in pleading for their daughter's return. Everyone in town also showed up, wanting answers about why all the questions had been asked. People who hadn't been asked themselves but heard about the police activity were as eager as everyone else.

"Thank you all for coming today," the sheriff began. "I know you want answers on why all the questions you all have been asked. You are probably wondering, why all the state police cars? Today you will have all your answers." The sheriff then motioned Joseph and

Margaret O'Connor to the front. "You all know Joseph and Margaret O'Connor?"

Taking his wife's hand into his, Joseph stepped up to the podium and said, "Twelve days ago, Katie, mysteriously disappeared..."

The crowd went wild with questions. The locals were upset about not being told from the start about Katie. She was one of them! Loved by all!

"Do you know if Katie is alive?" a reporter from their local paper, *The Gazette*, called out.

"What about Charlie? Does he have anything to do about this?" another from *The Gazette* asked.

"Have you received any phone calls? For ransom?" one of the news stations asked.

These were just a few of the questions asked by the reporters.

The sheriff stepped up to the mic, "Please, let Joseph continue, and then we'll take questions."

"As I was saying, Katie disappeared from work on the fourteenth. We have not heard from her since. This should explain all the questioning. Anybody who knows anything, or might have heard anything, please come forward. If you want to stay anonymous, that's fine. We'll abide by any of your wishes. We just want Katie back! Katie, wherever you are, please come home."

"*Please*, I just want my Katie home!" Margaret cried out.

The sheriff then took over, ready to answer any questions, "To answer some of your questions, we've not received any phone calls or received any ransom notes.

One person who was hanging far back in the crowd was Jack Hayes. Since the street was filled with people, no one paid attention or wondered why he was there. Everyone there was hoping for the best that the O'Connor girl would be found, all except Jack. He just wanted to gather information on how much the police knew and that his little secret was still safe.

After the press conference, reporters and townspeople stormed the department. Thousands of tips were given, some good, some bad. Lots had nothing to do with the case. But each piece of information had to be examined. Two troopers were assigned just to handle the job of sorting through every note and deciding which was good and which was bad.

On the news that one of their own, someone they all loved, was missing, the whole town wanted to help. Several of the O'Connors' friends went out on their own all over the county, searching.

When he left the conference, Jack went straight to his friend's. Freddy Gates knew everything. They, best of friends, were always hanging out together.

"Hey, man, I've not seen you in a while! What you been up too?" Freddy asked. "You've missed all the excitement around here!"

"What excitement? What have I missed?" Jack asked.

"The O'Connor girl is missing!" Freddy quickly answered.

"What the hell! What you mean by missing?" Jack trying to get information. "What have you heard?"

"Not much. Nobody knows anything. I just found out today when they had that press conference. Have you seen all the flyers being posted all over town? Even the state police is here."

"Nah, I never look at that shit. You say the state police is here?" Jack was leading Freddy on to get more information.

"Yeah, the state police! The sheriff has been up and down the street, talking to everybody. He even stopped here at my house, wanting to know if I heard or saw anything strange that might have happened around the store. Today, at the meeting, it explains all the questions."

"Well, did you?" Jack anxiously asked.

"Did I what?" Freddy answered.

"Did you see anything?" Jack was starting to get irritated.

"No, I mind my own business," Freddy answered, shaking his head.

Jack did not let on that he already knew about the conference and was there earlier that morning. He also did not mention about the sheriff coming out to his place.

"Hey, buddy, let's go have and drink and catch up. I've been so busy at home and decided to make time and get out today."

Together they walked up to the saloon, their favorite bar.

As they both entered the bar, a news report about the missing O'Connor girl interrupted all the programs and came alive on all channels. Everyone in the bar stopped their talking and listened to the report. Jack and Freddy went up to one of the TVs to get a closer look. Jack, of course, heard all this earlier and pretended to be just as interested as the others.

"Just think, we just saw her the other day out front of her daddy's store," Jack said to his friend.

"It says she's been missing close to two weeks. I remember the sheriff coming around, asking all these questions about the store. I just thought it was a break-in or something," Freddy added.

When the news broadcast was over, everyone in the bar continued their drinking and were all in deep conversation of what they thought about the missing girl.

One person was heard saying, "I bet she was pregnant, and her folks sent her away. This missing-person stuff is probably all fake to hide the truth!"

Another drinker implied, "I thought I saw her hitchhiking down I-69!"

Jack heard all these responses and just laughed.

Several shots later, he asked, "Do you know of anyone wanting help? I need some cash."

"Yeah, Gordon, out on I-69. I hear he is looking for someone to do some odd jobs around the house before he leaves on his trip. I hear he is going hunting in September."

Freddy changed the subject, "Goddamn, you're in a good mood! I know I've not seen you in weeks, but you've not been this happy in a long time. What's going on, you get cha a little tail? Anyone I know?" Freddy joked, laughing.

"You shut your mouth!" Jack shouted at his friend.

"Easy! I didn't mean anything! Calm the fuck down! If you want to keep her to yourself, no big deal! I've got my Allie."

Draining the rest of his whiskey, Freddy slammed the glass on the counter. He headed out for his long walk back to his house.

Now knowing James Gordon was needing help, Jack threw some bills on the counter to pay for the drinks, went down the street to collect his car, and headed that way. He didn't think how late it was. Even though he needed the money, he hoped this job wouldn't take too much time away from his sweet thing.

Thirty minutes later, as he drove down the Gordon's lane, Jack saw a beautiful log cabin nestled back in the hills, a two-story cabin with a wraparound porch.

"Damn, I'd like to live in something like this!" he said to himself out loud.

Parking his beat-up old Ford, he ventured up the steps and rang the doorbell.

Teresa, James's wife of thirty years, came out of their bedroom.

"Who could be visiting us at this hour?" she asked her husband.

"I'll see. Go on to bed. I'll be there shortly," James told her as he got up off the sofa. "Do you know what time it is? Who comes calling this late?" Gordon shouted while answering the door.

"Mr. Gordon, I am sorry, I didn't realize how late it was. My name is Jack Hayes. I heard you might be needing help?"

"Where'd you hear that?" James asked.

"You know Freddy…Fred Gates? He told me something about it," Jack hurriedly answered.

"Yes, I know Fred. He sent you to see me?"

"Yeah! I need a little cash. I'm a handyman of sorts and can do about anything thrown at me," Jack answered.

"I guess Fred's an okay guy. Drinks a little too much to suit me. A beer every now and then is okay, but he tends to take it a little too far. That's my opinion! Come in," James said as he allowed Jack to enter through the door. "I need to tell my wife where I'll be."

Leaving Jack alone in the living room, James went toward the master bedroom. Left alone, Jack admired what all was in the room: a deer head mounted above the beautiful stone fireplace with a bear rug laying in front; several mounted large-mouth bass covered another. *Damn!* Jack thought with envy.

"Told her…" James said as he reentered the room. Seeing Jack admire his prized trophies, he asked, "Do you, too, enjoy the sport?"

"Not really," Jack answered. "I don't have the time! Wish I did though. You have some beauties!"

"Yep, I am quite proud of them all!" As they headed out the backdoor, James spoke up, "I'll show you what I want done and see if we can agree on the cost."

As they entered the garage, Jack saw the expensive bass boat and said, "Boy oh boy! What a beautiful boat!" as he ran his hand down the side.

"My wife calls her my mistress!" James said, laughing. "I spend more time on her than my wife!"

Joining the laughter, Jack said, "I hear ya! I spend a lot of my time out in my barn working with wood. I love building things: rockers, windmills, name it, I can build it. My wife doesn't understand about we men with our toys!" Jack continued in his laugh.

"How true! How about a beer?" James opened a small fridge behind the work bench, tossing a cold one to Jack.

"Now you're talking," he said as he pulled the tab. "I can't stay too late and upset my woman!" Jack stated, thinking of his woman at home…not his wife.

As they finished talking and got down to business, the work that was to be done and at what cost were finally agreed upon between the two. No set hours as long as the work was completed within six weeks. James wanted an office built in the far corner of his garage. Jack, not wanting to be away from home too long each day, thought it was perfect. James Gordon had a lifestyle Jack so desperately wanted but didn't want to work hard to get it. Driving home, Jack was anxious to see his lady.

Charlie got in touch with his friends and gave them the news of Katie. All of them, worried with him, agreed to help him look for her. They went around to his and Katie's favorite spots: the fishing hole where she and Charlie swam; the one-room shack deep in the woods of the mountains, pretending it was their home. It used to be a ranger station outside the park, but after new stations were built, the building was no longer needed. It was left abandoned and in ruins. All these memories brought tears to Charlie's eyes. How he loved that girl! Wanted to marry her! He had a good job with his father and made a decent wage that he and Katie could live on. He knew how much she cared for people; she still could have gone to school, but near home in Albuquerque, as a married woman. He did not want to stand in her way; he just wanted to be included. He remembered the big fight after she came home from her trip. Katie was not making any time for him.

When she came home from her cruise, she was a changed person. After seeing the hungry and homeless people in the world, Katie wanted to start helping right away. She worked both Saturdays and Sundays at the homeless shelter. Working in the kitchens, she served lunch and dinner meals to those in need. Standing on her feet and working those long, long hours, Katie, dead on her feet, would cancel her date with Charlie. She did this on many occasions. When she wasn't helping out in the kitchen, she would also hit the streets, looking for any unwanted clothing, shoes, or coats. Even toys for the little ones, she'd gather for the needy. Driving to all the surrounding towns, Katie was determined to help, leaving no time for Charlie.

She knew what he wanted, and Katie kept telling him she was not ready to settle down. She wanted to live first and travel! She had to try to help those in need! He remembered all the awful names he called her, knowing he really did not mean them: "bitch! Prick, tease!" In the end, Charlie had made it easy for Katie to just walk away.

It was getting late.

"Jackie, it's time for bed," Maddy said, kissing her on the forehead.

"Okay, Mommy. Will you read me a story?"

"Of course! Don't I always? Get your bath and find me what book you want read to you. Now scoot!" Maddy laughed, patting Jackie on the behind.

Laughing, Jackie went to get her pajamas and start her bath. Maddy wanted so desperately to keep her daughter away from the hurt. She loved her little girl so much! Jack, having very little to do with her, left it all on her shoulders: birthdays, Christmases. She tried to give her daughter a normal life. It was a good thing Jackie was such a good girl. She never wanted much and was happy with what she did get.

Getting paper dolls cut out of old newspapers and handmade necklaces or bracelets out of pebbles Maddy would find in the desert were some of the gifts given to her for her birthday. Christmas was harder for her to find or make a gift. One Christmas Maddy took her own brush and mirror set that she had stored away and shined them, making them look good as new. She had Jackie believe they were bought at the store by her daddy. The secrets she had to keep!

Each year they both looked for the perfect tree. The perfect-shaped cacti! Both she and Jackie would drape it in blankets and would, with heavy work gloves, drag it into the house. It made Maddy so happy, seeing her daughter all in giggles, decorating it, stringing popcorn and berries, and covering it with homemade ornaments. Maddy tried to make each holiday better than the previous.

Maddy herself had not seen a birthday gift in years! She had not once had, "Happy birthday," said to her in the eleven years she was married! Birthdays were just another day to her.

The school was having their annual student conferences. Jack tried stopping her from going, but Maddy finally convinced him to let her go. Talking with her daughter's teacher, she found herself in disbelief. Her sweet little girl had no friends. Her teacher had informed her that Jackie would just sit under a tree at recess all alone. She would try to persuade her to join the others but had no luck! Maddy was also told that all her daughter's grades were dropping. No homework was being turned in. Notes were sent home daily to them, asking for a conference, but with no response! Jackie was always informing her teacher that her mother had no time to come in.

Maddy knew her little girl was quiet at home but didn't think anything about it. Hearing all that went on at school, or what wasn't going on, was unbelievable news to her. She thought to herself, *What a terrible mother I have become!* Well, it was going to change, starting today.

Half an hour later, after later Jackie's bath, and she was snuggled deep under her blankets, she waited for her nightly ritual, book-reading.

Jack never understood the bedtime ritual: book-reading and snuggling together. He always said, "She don't need that!" He just wanted her to go to bed and get out of his hair. He was a selfish man.

Maddy finished cleaning the kitchen and made sure everything met all of Jack's satisfaction, even though he was very seldom in the house anymore. Except for an occasional change of clothes, he began eating and sleeping elsewhere. Turning off the light, she joined her daughter.

With all the changes going on around them, Maddy decided to fix herself up a little using makeup and dressing better. She hoped to get Jack's approval and get things back to normal—whatever back to normal meant! But no response ever came from him.

"Now, before we read, there is something we need to talk about—school!"

Jackie buried her face in her pillow. She knew her mom had gone to school.

"Honey, please, we need to talk about this!" Turning her over to face her, Maddy continued, "Why haven't you told me about your troubles? You know you can come to me anytime and talk about anything! I'm sorry you're going through all this, this business between me and your father. I hope you know I will protect you from any harm that might come your way. You are safe at school, but you know nothing can ever be said about what is going on out here."

"Mommy, I know that. But I'm afraid for you! Daddy has hurt you so many times. I hate him so much!"

"Oh baby, I am sorry you feel that way. There's something wrong with Daddy that makes him act that way."

"Mommy! It's all my fault Katie is here!" she started to cry.

"It's not your fault! You just drop those thoughts right now! I will start being a better mommy and pay better attention to you."

"Mommy, you are already the *best* mommy ever!"

"Oh sweetheart. I love you so much! We will get through this! Somehow, we will get through this, I promise you! You've got to do better in school by doing your homework and bringing me any note from the teacher. Otherwise, someone from school might come out here, and that would not be good for any of us! Now, you promise me you will do your *best* and let me do all the worrying! *Promise*!"

"I promise, Mommy!" Jackie said. They hugged each other.

"Okay, now that's settled, what have you decided for us to read? How about *Rebecca of Sunny Brook Farm*?"

"No, Mommy, we finished that last week. Tonight I want to hear one of the *Nancy Drew* mysteries."

"*Nancy Drew* it is!"

Settling back on the bed beside her daughter, they took turns reading. Living so far out, Maddy kept a supply of books to keep her daughter occupied.

Joining a book club was her only salvation. Through a mailer, Maddy could buy used paperbacks for her daughter. Monthly the books would be delivered to their mailbox at the post office in town. When she went into town once a month to do the shopping, she'd pick up the mail. But with all the changes going on with Jack, she had to cancel the book-ordering since he took over the grocery-shopping and with money becoming so tight. Not that they had a lot before, it's just that he was drinking more and more, wasting any extra they might have had. He did not trust her going to town alone, so Maddy had not been away from the house since he brought Katie to their home. The only exception was the teacher conference. He knew he couldn't get out of that.

CHAPTER 8

The Nail

Weeks turned into months. The state police had nothing. No leads!

"Are you sure she didn't just take off with her boyfriend?" the lieutenant asked the sheriff for the hundredth time.

"He's still here in town, working, and says he knows nothing. I believe him. I've even had him followed to see where he goes and who he talks to. Nothing!"

"Yes, we talked with him too," the lieutenant added. "We went hard at him, hoping he'd slip and say something. I, too, think he's in the clear. We keep coming up with nothing! It's going on six months. I need that list of customers again that were in the store the week she worked. I want to go over it again in case I missed something. It's just a shame the camera was down that week. That would have helped tremendously!"

"I know! It was kinda slow that week. Here is what I come up with through charge-card receipts and customer invoices. But the ones who paid cash, we have no idea who they might be." Looking through his notes, the sheriff added, "James Gordon was in two or three times that week. It was unusual for him to be in town so many times in the same week since he lived so far out of town. I talked to him about those visits, and he explained that he needed the items that were special ordered and wanted to pick them up before he forgot. It made sense. Gordon is a regular in the store and good friend of the family."

"Well, I want to talk to him again. You never know about friends…maybe had a thing for their daughter!" Lieutenant Reynolds added as he looked through the list of names.

Alone, Katie looked all around the room. The room with only one window, she was able to look outside what little she could see. The shackle was still on her ankle; he at least made the chain long enough to reach her sink and toilet area. She shuddered every time she had to use that bucket. The stench coming from it was horrendous. The bucket, if lucky, was dumped every two or three days when

Jack remembered. Katie found an old burlap bag and draped it over it to help hold back some of the smell. Dealing with her monthly flow was disastrous! No tampons! No pads! She had to handle the situation each month the best she could. She used old rags she found in the potato bins. Even though she rinsed them out several times a day to cover herself, it still made her feel dirty all the time! Seeing her face in the cracked mirror, she could barely recognize herself. A black eye, a swollen lip, and her body was badly bruised. She tried to clean up in the little sink the best she could. Her hair, bloody from the beatings, was uncombed. How she wished to be back home in her tub full of bubbles.

Every day and night Jack abused Katie. The only time he left her alone was when she had her monthly. When she wouldn't do what he requested, he would hit her. She knew she had to get through this day by day. She was always searching for anything that could be used as a weapon to protect herself, or even help her to escape.

One morning, while looking out the window, Katie caught a glance of something shiny in the windowsill. A nail!

"I found a nail!"

Katie started laughing. How crazy is was to be excited over a stupid nail! She had to be losing her mind! Thinking maybe that nail could help her get out of here, she sat back down on the bed, smiling, the first time in months. Hearing the jiggling of the lock, Katie knew her peace was over. Finding a tear in the mattress, she secretly hid the nail inside the stuffing.

"Honey, I need my sleeping pill!" Jack announced, smiling as he came in through the door.

After a quick assault on Katie, he rolled over on his side and fell asleep. Waking early the next morning, he went up to the house to get their breakfast.

Katie always thought herself to be a strong person and could conquer anything. She tried to think of ways she could defend herself against Jack Hayes. But he always overpowered her with his strength. While he laid beside her at night, sleeping, she'd try to slip out from under his body in her attempt to get away, but he'd wake and pull her closer, making it hard for her to even move. He was so big and strong he could always control her. But she knew a day would come…

After he left, she retrieved her precious nail. As she rolled it around in her hand, she thought to herself, there was a light at the end of the tunnel.

The sheriff was at the O'Connors, giving them an update on the investigation—which was nothing! It was like Kaitlyn O'Connor just dropped off the face of the earth.

"Honey, I don't know what else to do!" Joseph said, holding his wife. "We have to go on with our lives. For our sanity!"

"I know! It's been over six months! The holidays we missed! Thanksgiving, Christmas, her birthday! *We missed her nineteenth birthday!*" Margaret cried out. "It's so hard to stop hoping!"

Christmas presents were stacked in a corner, waiting for Katie to unwrap.

"I will never stop hoping or looking!" the sheriff stated. Led to the door by Joseph, he continued, "Until we find her, the case will never be closed! I will never stop working it. Someone will slip up, and I will be there!"

With nothing leading the state police toward a possible kidnapping, they just closed their files and left, treating it as a runaway. There was never a ransom note, so kidnapping was ruled out. They could not find anyone that might have seen or heard anything. The town still tried to help; Katie was their little girl. Flyers were placed all around in surrounding towns, and the sheriff kept in constant contact with all the other police departments. News broadcasts flashed on all television channels all day and late into the night. Nothing surfaced. The troopers, having gone through all the tips, found nothing that could lead them in the right direction. With her being of age, nothing could really be done.

CHAPTER 9

Rods and Reels

Margaret was now working in the store with Joseph. She hated to be at the house all alone and decided to join the workforce. Joseph did not realize what an asset she was to him and the store. Greeting the customers as they entered, she would always ask about their spouse and children then helped them in their shopping. Before, just the men came in; but with Margaret working, the women soon accompanied their spouses just to visit with Margaret while the men did their shopping. In catalogs Margaret showed them all the new colors of clothing and the different rod and reels for women. Seeing all their interests, Margaret suggested that the store start stocking all kinds of accessories for women also. Clothing in bright colors, which included camo jackets and overalls in pink, filled the show floor.

Fishing equipment designed for women, including rod and reels and tackle boxes in an abundance of colors, now sat on the shelves. Who would have guessed the women would enjoy hunting or fishing with their partner? And the women did not realize how much fun it was!

Working at the store gave Margaret new meaning. She was excited again and eager to start her day. She came up with all kinds of ideas that included women. She still thought of Katie.

Was she okay? Would her baby girl ever come home?

Working together also brought Joseph and Margaret closer. Wives, girlfriends joined their significant others and were no longer fighting about their partner spending too much money on things they thought they did not need. They now found themselves spending just as much, if not more, on the same accessories. It was a win-win for all: the men, their significant other, and the store!

As things were getting better for the O'Connors, it was not for Maddy. She tried and tried to get closer to Jack, but he very seldom talked to her, only to tell her when to fix their meals or yell at her when something wasn't right. He'd clean up, sometimes shower, then leave. He had stopped sleeping in the house. Even though Jack hadn't slept with Maddy in years, he was at least in the house. He would always get so drunk in the evenings and just fall asleep in his chair every night, snoring in his stupor.

One day she caught him going through her things.

"Jack, what are you doing?"

"I need to find some clean clothes for my Katie." Looking through her closet, he threw clothing all over the room. Next he went through to her dresser. "Is this all you got?" he asked, holding up worn undergarments. "You can't even wear half of these things anymore," he said as he threw them on the floor.

Maddy quickly picked up the discarded things.

"What did you expect? You've not bought me or Jackie anything in years! I mend my tops and slacks, and poor Jackie has to wear my made-over dresses and tops to school."

"Why should I care? Look at yourself! You're nothing but a *fat cow!* I can barely look at you!" Jack shouted as he turned back to the dresser.

"I have to get my girl new things. I'll not go into work until late tomorrow, and we are going shopping, just you and me. You can pick out some pretty things for me. It won't look right, me buying women clothes, so you will do it for me."

"You've *got* to be kidding!"

"Yes, you will!" he snarled, jerking her around to face him. "You will do exactly as I say."

"Of course, Jack, as you say. What about Jackie? Will she be joining our *family outing* tomorrow?" Maddy snapped, starting to find her voice and saying her piece.

"No! She can stay here. We won't be gone long."

Jackie, leaning against the door facing just inside her bedroom, heard what had transpired between her parents.

Early the next morning Jack and his wife prepared for their journey into town. It had been several months since Maddy was able to leave the house. Ever since Jack brought home the O'Connor girl, he did all the shopping. She'd give him a list, but he still got all the wrong things: olive oil instead of vegetable oil; butter milk instead of regular milk for Jackie. The carton of eggs he purchased always had several ones cracked inside. Nothing was right. She had to make do with what he brought home, then he would complain about that evening meal. It was a blessing to get out and stock up on all she needed.

"Now, little girl, you *will* stay in the house! We will not be gone long, a couple hours at the most!" Jack told his daughter.

"Yes, Daddy," Jackie said, cowering behind her mother.

Maddy kissed her on the forehead, got in the car, and Jack sped off, barely giving Maddy time to pull the door shut.

Jackie, left alone in the house, picked up her favorite doll and hugged it close. Waiting a few minutes, and against her daddy's orders, she took her coat and ran toward the cellar, knowing exactly where it was. She used to play there all the time, making believe she was in school. She made her own school room by using old wooden crates to make her desk and stacked her books and old magazines on baskets. She pretended to be the teacher, using her dolls and stuffed animals as students. She told her mommy she didn't need anyone to play with, but the truth was, she did! She missed having a friend! But having a friend meant talking with them and sharing secrets. She was so afraid to talk with anyone she might accidently let that one deadly secret she had slip out, telling someone what was going on at her home.

Having to remove snow and ice off the doors before she could get them open, she was finally able to walk down the snow-covered steps that led down below the ground to the cellar. She was stopped by another door that prevented her from entering the room. The door, which Jack had installed before taking Katie, also had a huge lock. She could not get in with that there. Gently knocking on the door, Jackie listened for any response.

Then, knocking harder, Jackie called out, "Katie! Katie! Can you hear me?"

"Who's there?" Katie responded as she jumped off the bed and headed toward the door.

The chain on her ankle only allowed her to get so close to the door. Three feet from the door was the closest she could get to it. She could just barely hear the voice on the other side.

"It's me, Jackie! I'm so sorry I did this to you!"

"Are you alone?"

"Yes, Mommy and Daddy went into town. I'm all by myself."

"Can you open the door?"

"No! There's a big lock on it. I'm not supposed to be here, but I had to see if you were all right. Are you okay?"

"I've got to get out of here. I have a chain on my ankle."

"I'm sorry!" Jackie cried, running back to the house. She could not stay any longer, knowing she could not get that lock open.

"Jackie! Jackie! Don't leave me!" Katie screamed as she hit her fist on the ground.

The drive to Albuquerque was quiet. Maddy could almost hear her heart beat out of her chest. She said not one word to Jack and just looked out the window, seeing all the usual sights: cacti and miles and miles of desert. Sitting there beside him, she tried to figure out what her husband was up to.

Entering town, Jack drove straight to the sporting-goods store.

"You've got to be kidding!" Maddy screamed at her husband.

"What better way to dress my lovely than with her own daddy's clothes," said Jack, laughing. "Just remember *we* are a *happy* couple shopping!"

Finding a parking space in the back row of the lot, Jack led the way toward the front of the store. In the cold, January wind, Maddy, all bundled up, was slowly following. Entering through the door first, he waited for his wife to catch up. Jack saw Margaret O'Connor immediately, talking with another couple.

"Come on, let's introduce ourselves," he said, pulling Maddy behind him.

Turning her attention to the approaching couple, "Hello! Welcome to our store! Have we met before?" Margaret greeted them, shaking Jack's hand and hugging Maddy.

"No, this is our first time in the store. We live out by the mountains a few miles from here and don't get into town much, but my wife," said Jack, hugging and pulling her close, "needs some new things. You know how women are always wanting something. I've put her off long enough."

"Come with me, and I'll help," Margaret said, leading Maddy toward the women's section.

"Hon, don't be too long…and *remember* what we talked about!" He glared at her as Jack warned his wife. "I'll stay back here and wait, say, fifteen, twenty minutes?"

"Silly!" Margaret answered him, "It'll take longer than that. Now what size are we thinking, ten…twelve?"

Looking back toward Jack, she said, "No, I need about a six."

"Six?" Margaret puzzled. "But you look about…."

"No, I have plans to lose weight. I need these things to keep me on track for my goal. I want to get down to a size 6."

"Well, okay then, we better get crackin' before your husband storms over here," Margaret said, laughing.

After what seemed like forever, Maddy had all her items. Margaret went ahead toward the front, leaving Maddy to browse on her own. She picked up a top and jeans for herself, in her size, and hurriedly ran to the children's section and grabbed items for Jackie: a couple dresses and undergarments. She knew she'd not get another opportunity to do this. Taking all her items, she headed toward the checkout center.

Jack joined her, taking her forearm.

"You didn't say anything, did you, woman?" he asked her in a low voice.

"No, Jack. I did just like you told me."

"Good! *What* all did you buy, sweetheart?" he asked, seeing the total.

It was costing more than he realized as he counted out the cash. If this kept on, he'd soon be broke before his next draw from Gordon. It was a good thing he knew people and got discounts on the lumber he bought to finish the job. He also knew how to "work around things."

"*Babe!* You told me to get all that I needed. With the pounds I plan to lose, silly, I'll need all new undergarments too," Maddy said, hugging him around the waist.

Jack glared at her and said, "I guess I did say that, didn't I, sweetie?" After he paid the bill and started gathering the bags, he turned to Margaret, "How's that daughter of yours? Isn't her name Kaitlyn? She's such a sweet thing, all grown up!"

"What?" Margaret asked, immediately tearing up.

Hearing this, Maddy thought she would pass out. She just stormed out to the car, with Jack soon catching up.

"Did you see her face?" Jack asked, laughing.

"Jack! How could you be so mean?" Maddy could not believe Jack would do such a thing.

"Me! Mean? I don't have a mean bone in my body," he said, turning her around to face him. "If you pull that stunt again, so help me." He slapped her in the face and growled, "Now get in the car!" as he threw the door open.

Maddy knew what he was talking about. He must have seen the extra items of clothing for herself and Jackie in the mix. She had to take the chance. She thought she got away with it and would probably pay for it when they got home. It was worth the beating to come. She had not had anything new for herself and Jackie in a long time. She couldn't wait to see Jackie's excitement.

Before heading for home, they made a second stop at the grocery. More money was spent buying groceries, leaving Jack with only a few dollars remaining from his pay from Gordon. He'll just have to tell old-man Gordon he miscalculated on a few things and needed a few more bucks. He'll tell him he can take it out of his final pay.

On the drive home, Jack thought of how he was gonna present his sweet thing with all her new pretties, knowing how excited she would be. How would she pay him back? Licking his lips, pushing the pedal down, he wanted to get home soon as possible. Maddy again was very quiet, leaning against the car door and wanting this day to be over.

Even before the car come to a complete stop, Maddy was out the door, running into the house.

"Jackie, sweetie, where are you?"

Coming out of her room, she appeared, still holding her baby doll.

"Mommy, here I am. I was just reading my books all day."

"Honey, you must be hungry, let me start lunch," Maddy said, showing her concern. It was after 2:00.

"While you do that, fix me a couple plates too. Make it something special 'cause my gal will be so happy when she sees all the pretty things I bought for her," Jack ordered as he came inside.

"Yes, Jack! Will there be anything else you *desire?*" she asked, quickly putting away the groceries before starting the late lunch.

Pulling out a pot, she decided to have spaghetti and meatballs, one of Jackie's favorite meals. Finally, with her visit to the store, Maddy was able to stock up on other foods besides having hamburgers or canned soup all the time, which Jack seemed to always buy, along with the wrong items he picked up instead of what was on the list. Keeping the costs down, Maddy knew what to buy and at great savings: pasta, spaghetti, hot dogs, and other quick meals that Jackie liked. She was the only one Maddy loved to cook for.

"You better watch that tongue! I've not forgotten what you pulled today! All those extra clothes you added. I saw the things that were in Jackie's size," Jack barked, hitting the fridge as he paced back and forth, waiting on his plates.

After Jackie left, Katie worked all morning, using the nail to dig around the windowsill.

Hearing the door being unlocked, she jumped down off the chair, hid her prized possession, and waited.

So excited to show Katie his gifts, Jack should have noticed the cellar doors were clearer of snow, but they did not faze him. His mind was on other things.

"Baby, did you miss me? I have a surprise for you!" Jack exclaimed as he entered the room and laid several bags on the bed.

Seeing the bags and knowing where they came from made Katie cry out hysterically, "How could you?"

"Baby, don't cry! I thought you'd be happy getting familiar things. Hell! What does it take to please you women!" He threw the bags at her and yelled, "You can think it over and realize why I did it." He exited the room.

Katie took the clothes and held them close as she cried.

Not bothering to collect their meal, Jack got back in his car and drove off. He had to get to work. He needed the money now from all that spending he did today. Everything cost more than he had expected, the clothes, the groceries. *Hell with it!* he thought. Instead of going out to the Gordon's, he went straight to Freddy's.

"I'll catch up work tomorrow," he said, talking to himself. "Gordon don't care when or how often I work long as I finish the job on time."

Hearing the car drive off, Maddy called for Jackie to join her in the bedroom.

"Mommy, you need me?" Jackie answered, joining her mom in the bedroom.

"Let me show you what I bought for you today before we eat. Sit beside me," she said, patting the bed beside her. She then held up two dresses

"Oh Mommy, they're so pretty!" Jackie exclaimed, holding one of them up to her.

"I know they're a little big, but if we take good care of them, they should last a long time. I don't know the next time I can go shopping again. Look, I also got you undies," she said, holding up the packages of *The Little Mermaid* underwear.

"Oh Mommy, you got something too!" she said, looking over the top and jeans laying on the bed. Running the top's material through her fingers, she said, "It feels so soft! You will be the prettiest mommy in the world."

The top was just a regular flannel shirt, but new. Seeing Jackie's excitement, it showed Maddy how long it had been since anything new was bought for either of them. She would cut down and hem old shirts of Jack's for herself and sewed her old tops to fit Jackie. Tears formed in her eyes, seeing what a special little girl she had, hearing the excitement in her daughter's voice over her mommy's new items rather than her own. They just sat there and hugged.

"Come on, let's fix dinner, do dishes, and get ready for bed. I hear a book calling our names, wanting to be read."

Jumping off the bed, Jackie headed for the kitchen with her mother following.

With all that was happening with Jack, Jackie's birthday passed this year with no gift or birthday cake. Jackie did not remember anyway when her birthday was. But Christmas was different. This year she found tiny cacti plants and small stones she dug out of the snow to make a terrarium for her daughter. Jackie was so excited, seeing something so pretty, and placed it on the windowsill in her bedroom.

Katie, with puffy eyes from crying all night, continued her slow process of digging all around the window. Making a good start, she cleaned up her mess and sat back on her bed. Her fingers were raw and bleeding from all the scraping she did that morning. Running cold water over them made them sting with more pain. Having accomplished a lot today, she was proud! Hopeful!

CHAPTER 10

Newfound Friends

Jack woke the next morning in great pain. What the hell did he drink last night? Sitting up, he grabbed his head.

"Oh my god! How much did we drink last night?"

It became late that previous evening; he just stayed the night.

Freddy entered the front room very slowly.

"I don't know about you, but…I feel like hell," he said as he saw all the beer cans and empty tequila bottles all over the floor. "You certainly were in a foul mood when you got here yesterday. I don't know what set you off, but you were way out there!"

Jack also saw all the empty bottles scattered everywhere and remembered exactly what went on yesterday. "See you later," was all he said, getting up and heading for the door.

"Hey! You gonna help me clean up this mess?" Freddy asked Jack as he pointed out all the bottles and cans lying around. Jack waved him off as he went out the door toward his car.

"Thanks for nothing, asshole!" Freddy shouted as he started throwing bottles in a trash bag.

Jack, forgetting all about his promise to himself about going to work, drove home instead. As he made it home in record time, even on the icy, snow-covered roads, he drove straight toward the cellar. Leaving a path in the snow, he hurriedly unlocked the door and bolted in. Grabbing Katie under the blankets, he plowed into her over and over. Katie screamed. This was the worst she was ever treated. Trying to pull away, Jack slapped her in the face and plunged deeper and faster into her. Finally coming to his senses, he stopped and raised himself off her body. Straightening his clothes, he left just as fast as he came in, leaving Katie to herself.

Grabbing the blanket off the floor, she curled up in a fetal position, crying, wishing she was dead. Each day was getting worse than the day before. She had to get away from there!

Jack stumbled into the house, slamming the front door behind him and yelling, "Maddy!"

Entering the room after hearing all the commotion, "Lower your voice!" she ordered, seeing Jackie sitting on her bed in her room through her open door.

"You women are all alike! Want, want, want! Don't you think I'm letting you get away with that stunt you pulled in town yesterday," Jack snarled, grabbing her by the shoulders. "Nobody makes a fool out of Jack Hayes!" he shouted, shaking her.

"Daddy! Stop!" Jackie cried, running to them.

Turning toward her, he said, "Don't you start, little girl! Or you will get the same!"

He released Maddy and shoved her away. As she fell to the floor, Jack gave her a swift kick to the stomach before storming into the bedroom, slamming the door behind him.

Jackie ran to her mother lying on the floor and helped her to a chair. Maddy saw the shape Jack was in, smelling strong of liquor, and realized his temper was getting worse. What more was yet to come?

Joseph noticed how shaken Margaret had gotten before she left the store. Something must have happened. She said an emergency had come up and had to leave. Joseph was about to ask if he could help but quickly realized she was already gone. When he got home that evening, it was totally dark in the house, not a single light on, and supper was not started. He wondered if Margaret was even home. But seeing her car in the garage told him she was unless she had gone out with someone. As he searched the house, he found her fast asleep on their daughter's bed, holding Katie's picture to her chest. She hadn't done that in a long time. He thought she was healing. Covering her with a blanket, he left her there to sleep the night. After making himself a sandwich, Joseph went on to their bedroom alone.

Before leaving for work the next morning, he gently knocked on the door of their daughter's room. Seeing his wife was still asleep, he just kissed her on the cheek and left her sleeping. He would wait until later to address the issue.

At work, in the morning meeting, Joseph asked his employees if anything unusual happened the day before.

"Yes, I heard something," Tony, one of the cashiers, spoke up. "Mrs. O'Connor was helping a lady shop, and as they were checking out, the husband said something about Katie. Whatever the conversation was, it rattled Mrs. O'Connor."

"Did you know the couple? Have they shopped here before?" Joseph asked his employee.

"I didn't hear much, only Katie's name being mentioned. This is the first time I've seen them here in the store, but I have seen him around town," Tony answered.

"Why don't you pull the video of that time yesterday and bring it to me. There better not be a problem with it this time! Get it to me ASAP," Joseph insisted, feeling tense.

"Will do, Mr. O'Connor, right away," Tony said, making a note on his steno pad.

"This is so strange! Everyone in town knows what is going on and that Katie is still missing. Okay, guys, that's all for today. Have a good day!" Joseph said, concluding the meeting. "Just bring me that tape!" Joseph reminded Tony before returning to his office.

Margaret finally woke, turned, and looked around the room. Seeing all of Katie's personal items brought back tears. All the pictures of her and her friends were all around the room. And still on the dresser was a picture of Charlie with his big smile. Makeup was scattered all over her vanity, just as she had left it that Friday morning. She was still gone! No word! The pain would never go away. They were trying to get on with their lives. Working with her husband helped. She found that she enjoyed working at the store. It gave her a new purpose to live! As she rose off the bed, she went to shower before going into work.

As she made herself get up, aching from the violent attack she had just received, Katie went to the sink to clean up. As she looked in the mirror, she saw a bruised, swollen face, her hair covered in blood. Her captor was getting more and more vicious. Taking a cold cloth, she gently wiped the blood away from her lip and nose. Taking her tool out from its hiding place, she continued her work. She was not going to let the beatings stop her. She scratched and scratched, scraped and scraped all around the window. Her knuckles again began to bleed. She got one of her rags to wrap around her hand and continued.

Later that afternoon Jack finally emerged from the bedroom.

Not bothering to shower or change clothes, he told Maddy, "I'm going into work for the rest of the day," and walked out the door.

Seeing the car drive off, Maddy called out to her daughter, "Jackie, sweetheart, I have to see if Kaitlyn is all right."

"Mommy, please don't. Daddy will find out! While you were away yesterday, I snuck out and talked to her," Jackie told her mother.

"You did! You know how dangerous that was for you to go out there against your daddy's warning. I don't like you doing that."

"But, Mommy, I had to! It's all my fault she is here," Jackie cried out to her mother.

"Remember me telling you it is not your fault? You did not know what your daddy was planning. He lied to you about why he wanted you with him," Maddy assured her daughter. "Let's go now. I have to know if she is okay."

Opening the back door, they both ran to where the cellar was hidden. Jackie led the way as they walked in the tire tracks Jack had made earlier.

Approaching the cellar and opening the doors, Jackie said, "Mommy, she's down there," and pointed down the steps.

Maddy saw the newly installed door. After jiggling the lock, she pounded hard against the door.

"Kaitlyn, are you okay?" she called out.

Hearing a voice, Katie jumped up.

"Jackie, is that you?" she asked.

"Yes, Katie, Mommy is with me. Daddy is gone."

"Kaitlyn, this is Madeline. Are you all right? Honey, I'm sorry this is happening to you."

"Madeline, I'm scared of what he's planning to do with me. He hurts me all the time! I am so ashamed of what he makes me do! The last time he hurt me really bad!"

"Honey, I feel it's all my fault. I just don't know what to do. Since the day we got married, his whole personality changed. He was such a sweet person then quickly turned into an awful monster. He is not the same man I thought I knew. If he found out I was talking to you, he'd kill me and hurt Jackie. He made me go into town with him and buy those things for you at your folk's store. He is so sick! The things he said to your momma, it was sad."

"He talked to Mom! Is she okay?" Katie asked.

"I don't know. She turned white as a sheet from what he said to her," Maddy replied.

"What about Daddy? Are they looking for me?" Katie hoped.

"I didn't see your daddy, but surely, they are looking for you, honey."

Katie sank to the floor, crying. She had never cried so much in her life. When would the horror end? Or would it ever!

"Katie, you have to be strong! I will think of something. Are you eating? You need to keep up your strength. I'll make sure you get lots to eat. With this huge lock on the door, I can't open it. I will try to figure out where he keeps the key, but I am sure it's always on him. Just pray! I'll think of something. He has a job he goes to each day, and Jackie and I will try to come back as often as we can," Madeline said through the door, trying to console her.

"That's all I do...pray! Please don't leave me!" Katie cried out.

"We'll come back. I won't let you be alone. I promise! I've got to get back to the house. Jack went to work for the rest of the day. It'll probably be late when he gets home. Hopefully, he will leave you alone tonight."

Katie knew they were gone. She just learned she had a friend and was not alone in this nightmare, someone to give her hope!

At Gordon's place, Jack finished hanging the last of the paneling in James's new office. After adding the final touches, he stood back and admired his work. When he did work, he did a great job! James surprised him as he entered the room, handing him a cold beer.

"You've done a fine job and finished way ahead of time too! I might just have some more work for you. With Christmas gone and spring around the corner, I need to start buttering up my wife to prepare her for my upcoming trip. Come with me, and I'll show you what I want done." As Jack followed him into the house, James showed him the way to the master bedroom. "Teresa has been wanting a walk-in closet for years. If you got the time, I've got the money!"

Finishing his beer, Jack smiled and said, "Lead the way, kind sir. I will most certainly make the time!"

After Maddy and Jackie left, Katie worked even harder at the window. A breeze was seeping through the cracks. The cold air made her take breaks to warm her hands at the heater many times while she worked. Even with it underground, it still got pretty chilly in the little room. Jack had brought in the small heater to help warm the room while he was there, but it didn't help much.

It was after midnight when Jack drove into the yard. Very pleased with himself, he was excited to see his gal and share the news. Katie heard the door and thought, *God! Please help me!* Covering herself and pretending to be asleep, she hoped Jack would leave her alone.

How wrong she was!

"Sweetie! Guess what? I got more work!" Jack announced, slapping her across the buttocks. "It's time to celebrate!"

Turning her to him, he started. Afterward Jack pulled her close to him and fell into a deep sleep.

Katie, hearing him snore, believed he was fast asleep. His strong body odor was unbearable. Trying to detach herself was impossible; when she was able to remove his arm from around her, he'd pull her closer. Her attempts were useless. She laid there with very little sleep until morning. As she felt the movement of his rising body, Katie carefully opened her eyes and watched his every move. When Jack turned to face her, she quickly closed them, pretending to still be asleep.

Jack thought to himself, a little fun before he left for work would help him start his day in the right way. He walked closer to her. Just as he was about to wake her, he changed his mind; he did not want to rush his lovemaking! He wanted all the time to enjoy every moment making love to his lady. Letting her sleep, he just left.

In the house, Jack told Maddy his plans while she fixed breakfast, "I have more work and should be gone most of the day. Remember what I said, to stay away from the cellar," taking the tray of food with him.

While he and Katie ate breakfast, he told her, "I hate being away from that beautiful body"—rubbing his hand up and down her thigh—"but work is calling me. Be sweet to me tonight, and maybe I'll get you something pretty to wear."

He gave her a big sloppy kiss before leaving for work.

As soon as Jack drove off, Maddy, ignoring the order, bundled up against the coldness and went to visit with Katie.

"Kaitlyn, can you hear me?"

"Madeline, I can just barely. Go around to the window where I can see you."

Hearing this, she ran around to the other side of the hillside, where the window was. Getting down on her hands and knees to the cold, snowy ground, she wiped it clear and was able to see Katie.

"Oh sweetheart," Maddy said, seeing her bruised face, "I've got to find a way to help you."

Standing on the chair, Katie was finally able to see another person for the first time in a long time. Her new friend!

"Can you hear me?" she asked, putting her hand up against the glass.

"Yes, I can. I feel for you. Jack is working in town today and said he'd be gone all day. We need to talk about a plan…of how to get you out of here."

"I've been working on this window, trying to dig out. I know it sounds like a stupid idea, but what else is there!"

Seeing the nail made Maddy realize how desperate Katie was to escape.

"Your poor fingers!"

Jack, a quarter of mile away, realized he had forgotten his toolbox. Turning around, he headed back home.

Maddy saw a car heading her way, "Katie, I've got to get back to the house, I see a car coming. Jack must be coming back." Before entering the house, she picked up a handful of wood to take into the house with her.

With the house in view, Jack saw what he thought was a person running up the porch steps and into the house.

"Goddamn it!" Coming to a stop and throwing the car in park, he stormed through the front door like a tornado. *"Madeline, where the fuck are you?"* he screamed, finding her coming out of the kitchen. "What did I say about going outside?"

"I was just getting more wood for the stove. Look at my hands and clothes," she said, showing him her muddy hands and clothes. "Besides, you didn't say anything about going outside, just to stay away from the root cellar."

"How long have you been disobeying me, woman?" Jack shouted at her.

"I have not disobeyed you. I'm just trying to keep this family alive! If that is what you call this—a family! Since you seem to have other things on your mind," Maddy spat at him.

"Don't you get smart with me!" He slapped her hard across the face, causing her to fall to the floor.

After kicking her in the face, he left the room.

Jackie heard all the shouting and waited for her father to leave before going to comfort her mother.

He grabbed his toolbox and put it in the trunk before slammed it shut. "Humm…I wonder what my wife really was doing!" As he walked toward the wood pile, he saw footprints on the snowy path leading out in the yard. Following them around the cellar entrance, they stopped at the window. He saw that it was wiped clear, and the ground beside it had footprints all around. As he got down on his knees he looked inside and found Katie looking straight at him.

"You bitch!"

Seeing Jack's face made Katie fall off the chair to the ground. The door opened.

The entire day Jackie sat with her mother. With a wet cloth, she patted the bruises all over her mother's face as she nursed her mother back to health.

Katie also needed comfort, but she was all alone! Her face was covered in blood, and one of her eyes was swollen shut. Laying on her bed, she cried softly to herself.

It was an unforgettable day!

CHAPTER 11

A Suspect

When Margaret entered the store, many eyes were on her.

"I'm late!" she called out to everyone. Joseph, hearing his wife's voice, went up to the front to meet her. "Honey, I'm sorry I'm so late," she told her husband after hugging him. "I had trouble getting up this morning."

"Darling, you didn't have to come in today. Take the day off and relax," Joseph told her as he walked with her to his office. "I heard a little of what happened yesterday. We need to talk about it."

"Oh, I was just being a baby! I have to be here working and keeping busy."

"I know, sweetheart. We will find her. Someone will mess up. I believe she is still alive, and I know you do too. We just need to have faith," Joseph insisted. "Did you know the couple that came in yesterday, and what exactly did he say to you?" Joseph went on to ask his wife.

"I never saw them before," Margaret answered. "But that poor woman, she was afraid to say anything without her husband's approval. I could tell she was terrified of him! They never gave me their name and paid with cash."

"Tony is pulling the video from yesterday's business, and we can see if I know them," Joseph went on to say.

"Our girl will come home to us. Now stop all this talk. I've got another idea. We need to start carrying…" Margaret said, shutting the door behind them.

Later that morning Tony brought in the video of the time period when the couple in question was cashing out into Joseph's office. Joseph input the disk into the computer and waited.

Margaret watched, ready to point out the correct couple.

"There, stop the film, this is the couple I helped yesterday.

Joseph waited patiently for the right moment to get a good look at the man's face. Finally, at the right moment, the male looked directly into the camera's view. What Joseph saw shocked him, and he immediately dialed the sheriff.

"Dave, you need to get over here now!" he shouted.

Joseph thanked his cashier, "Tony, that'll be all. You can get back to your station."

The sheriff rushed over to the sporting-goods store.

"You need to see this!" Joseph insisted.

The sheriff looked at the couple on the computer screen.

"What does this have to do with anything?" he asked.

"It's what he said to Margaret, something about Katie!" Joseph said, growing angry.

"Again, what does it have to do with Katie being missing?" the sheriff asked, confused.

"Don't you see, the way he is acting? Margaret said it's something about how he acted, so secretive. She also said the wife was buying clothes way too small for herself."

"Joseph, I'm sorry, but I don't see what this has to do with Katie. You're just grasping at straws! But to satisfy you, I will go out to the Hayeses again and look around. Maybe it was clothes for their little girl."

"Then why wasn't she with them?" Joseph wanted an answer.

"Like I said, I'll go out and pay them another visit," the sheriff concluded.

Later that week Sheriff Thomas, with one of his deputies, drove out to the Hayeses.

As they parked in front, he said, "Take a look around the place," pointing toward an old run-down barn. "Start with that," he ordered the deputy as he proceeded up the porch steps.

"Yes, sir!" the deputy answered, following the orders.

Maddy saw the car drive up and met him at the door.

"Sheriff, can I help you?" she asked as she dried her hands on her apron.

"Maddy, is Jack around?" the sheriff asked, removing his hat. "I need to talk to him a few minutes."

"No, Sheriff, he's working at James Gordon's."

"Yeah, I heard something about that. I hear he's doing a great job." Getting straight to the point of his visit, Dave said, "There's been some talk about the visit you both made in town a few days ago."

The sheriff saw shock appear on Maddy's face.

"What do you mean?" Maddy asked, struggling to get the words out.

"I'm talking about the conversation with Mrs. O'Connor," the sheriff answered.

"I didn't hear anything. I guess you need to talk with Jack about that. He won't be home until late," Maddy insisted on the conversation.

"I intend to! Just tell him to stop in the office tomorrow," said the sheriff.

"Will do, Sheriff."

"Maddy, are you and your little girl okay? How old is she now, ten, eleven?"

"Yes, we are fine. Thank you for asking. Jackie is eleven now."

In the back of her mind, Maddy wondered if she had the courage to say something to the sheriff, to save Kaitlyn and themselves. She remembered the beating from Jack and decided to keep her mouth shut. She was so frightened!

"Is that a bruise on your cheek?

"Yes, I slipped off the porch steps last week and hit the railing on my way to get wood."

"It looks to be more recent than a week ago!"

Maddy was about to disagree, but the sheriff went on, "Remember, if you need anything, I mean anything, Maddy, do not hesitate to come to me! I will help!"

"Thank you, Sheriff," she said, shutting the door.

With her back against the door, she started shaking. Why doesn't she have the courage to get help? She knew that answer, Jack!

Seeing his deputy already waiting beside the cruiser, Dave went to join him.

"You see anything unusual?" the sheriff asked.

"No, sir! I walked all around the house. That barn is about ready to collapse. It looks like it has never been kept up," the deputy replied.

"You sure you didn't see anything unusual?" the sheriff asked one more time.

"Positive!" the deputy clarified.

"Okay, let's head back to town," Dave said, both climbing in the car and leaving the premises.

The deputy failed to see the cellar at the back end of the yard, holding Kaitlyn O'Connor! And Kaitlyn did not know how close she was to being saved!

The following week Jack walked into the sheriff department.

"I heard you wanted to talk to me," he told the sheriff.

"It took you long enough! Come on back so we can talk in private."

"Have a seat," the sheriff said, taking his chair behind his desk and opened a file. "I hear that you and your wife were in O'Connor's Fish and Game store shopping last week.

"Yeah, I've been working and have money to spend! What of it? It is a free world, ain't it? My money is as good as the next person, ain't it?" Jack shouted out.

"Of course, it is," the sheriff answered back. "Why I am so concerned is the conversation you had with Margaret O'Connor. Something about her daughter. You do know she is missing?"

"I don't get into town much, so I didn't know she ran off. You know she isn't Miss Sweet and Innocent that she wants everyone to believe she is. I've seen the way she rubs up against that Watts boy and making out in the middle of the street!"

"Now is not the time to start lying to me by saying how little you come into town! I see your car either at Gates's house or parked in front of the bar at least three days a week. You had to have heard something?" The sheriff was getting aggravated. "I guess that is all I need to know. You can let yourself out," he said, standing. "Just remember to behave yourself, you and your buddy, Freddy. Any loud outbursts or interferences, I will run you in without batting an eye! Understand?"

"Yes, sir, your majesty! Am I free to go?" Jack asked, saluting the sheriff.

"Also, if I ever hear or see you hit your wife, I will bring you in and throw the key away. I'll also make sure you won't get out of jail until you're an old man! With or without your wife's consent! *Now*, get out of my face! You make me sick!" the sheriff shouted, fed up with his visitor.

As he hurried out the door, Jack took his handkerchief out of his pocket and wiped his forehead. He thought to himself, *That was too close!* He needed to make up a rumor to take any suspicion away from him and lead them to his good old buddy, and boss, James Gordon.

He was at the Gordon house every day, working on different projects. Jack would finish one job and would right afterward be given another. James, a few months away from his fishing trip, had lots to do, including securing the lodge.

"You did a wonderful job on my office, and I see you've almost finished my wife's closet. She is so excited about it and tells me so every day. I'd be proud to recommend you to anyone," James told him. Shaking his hand, he said, "Here's a little extra for your fine work." He handed Jack $500. "I might just keep you around here at the house, doing odd jobs, while I'm gone to help my wife if any crisis should arise."

"I'd be happy to, Mr. Gordon."

"Call me Jim."

"Jim it is!" Jack replied.

CHAPTER 12

Pregnant

January then February had come and gone, and soon it was spring. Katie kept track with marks on the wall like a calendar. She lost a day here and there when she was laid up from the beatings but felt she was close. Her birthday, which was last September, had come and gone with no celebration. Christmas gone...no presents. Life was just passing her by. She was supposed to start college months ago; it did not happen. She wondered if anyone at the college was worried about her no-show.

She worked and worked at the window. Since that awful day with Jack coming home and catching them all, Madeline had never been back. Knowing from her own beating, Madeline must have received one too.

Jackie was still sneaking out and visiting her whenever she could, usually every three days. Taking upon herself the chore of keeping the woodbox full in the house, this gave her the opportunity to go out to the root cellar and visit with her. Katie soon learned how smart her newly found friend was. They would sit and talk for a limited time before her mother, worried, would come looking for her. Jackie would talk only about her mother, nothing about school or her father. Katie would ask her something about him, where he worked, and Jackie would change the subject right away, not answering her question. Katie figured out immediately that Jackie had no friends at school. She talked about how happy she was for the school year coming to an end and not having to go back until after summer. Even with what was happening to her, being held captive, Katie felt sorry for the little girl.

Lately Katie would tire so easily and felt sick all the time. She had no idea what was wrong, thinking that she must have picked up a bug from the drafty window and dirty room. She had not felt this bad since middle school when she had an appendicitis attack.

For weeks Katie was feeling sicker and sicker. Just as she was waking, nausea would hit her, causing her to throw up.

"What is wrong with me?"

Being all alone, she could die! The smell of Jack's sweaty body would make Katie throw up.

Jack, seeing this, asked, "What is wrong with you? You sick?"

He didn't want another sickly person. He had that with his wife.

Never answering, she would just throw up again.

This went on for months. When the nausea finally stopped, Katie began to feel much better. Even though the bug had finally passed, Katie would still tire out easily and took several naps during the day.

The chain around Katie's ankle was becoming a nuisance and getting tangled up in her leg during "their lovemaking," so Jack started removing it then reattaching it that next morning before he left.

He was still taking her in the usual harsh way, but lately things did not feel the same. Her breasts felt bigger.

One afternoon, as he was taking the bucket out to dump, he got to thinking, when was the last time he saw a bloody mess? He knew women had this monthly ordeal. His wife was pitiful when she got hers and would lie around holding a pillow against her stomach. He would stay away when she went through that.

"What the hell!" he said, talking to himself. Hurrying back inside, He asked Katie, "Woman, when was the last time you had your monthly?"

Katie looked up at him.

Shock in her words, she cried, "I can't be!" She did not even think of that! "Please God, don't let it be true!"

"Son of a bitch!" Jack yelled out and threw the bucket against the wall. "Damn, damn, damn!" Jack shouted out. "This is all I need!" As he entered the house, he stormed into the kitchen area, yanking open all the cabinets, searching for a bottle. "I need a drink!" He could not find anything. What he did not know was, Maddy had thrown out all the liquor.

Jumping into his car, he hastily drove off. He did not slow down until he was halfway to town. Needing to think, he drove straight to his bar and ordered a beer with a shot of tequila. Downing the shot, he ordered another.

Freddy, sitting at a back table, saw Jack come in.

Walking up to the bar and taking the stool beside him, Freddy said, "I've not seen you in a while. Heard you were working at Gordon's."

"Give me what he's having?" he shouted to the bartender.

The bartender nodded and sat the drinks in front of him. Ignoring his friend, Jack just drank his drinks, not saying a word.

"Jacky, my boy, come join me and Alice at my table," Freddy said, pointing her out in the far corner. "You remember me telling you about Alice?" Freddy invited him.

"Not now, Freddy. I got things on my mind. Maybe later."

Downing the shot and swigging the beer, Freddy felt insulted and asked, "You getting too high and mighty to make time for me now, your buddy? Is hanging out with Gordon making you too good to remember your pals? Remember, I am the one who set you up."

"It's not that!" Jack said, assuring him. "I've just got things on my mind. Leave me alone."

"What about that sweet thing you have on the side?" Freddy shot at him.

Jack glared at him, "Shut your fucking mouth! You hear me! You know nothing of what I am going through! Nothing!" He threw some cash on the bar before storming out.

"What the hell!" Freddy shouted out, jumping off the stool, and headed out to follow Jack.

"Wait a minute! What about your bill?" the bartender informed him.

"Put it on my tab, I'll be right back. You know I'm good for it," Freddy assured him.

Alice rose from her chair and asked, "What about me?"

"Babe, I'll just be gone a few minutes. Have another drink, and I'll be back soon as I can."

Alice agreed and sat back down at the table and continued drinking.

Watching Jack drive off and keeping a safe distance, Freddy followed him out of town, toward his home. Stopping away from the house, he watched Jack drive his car around to the back.

"Where the fuck is he going?" Freddy asked himself. Leaving his car, he started walking in the direction Jack had parked. Keeping out of sight, he slowly crept around the house toward the car. He watched Jack lift what looked like doors and disappear down into the ground. "What the hell is going on!"

After Jack disappeared, Freddy ran up to the hillside. Finding a window, he peeked in, and what he saw, he could not believe his eyes—the O'Connor girl!

"*Fuck!*" What the hell was Jack doing with the girl? Seeing her condition and her lack of clothes, she had to have been there all along. For months! So that's his little secret, and he, Freddy Gates, wanted in. Scrambling to his feet and keeping out of sight, Freddy ran back to his car and headed back to town. Seeing the missing girl at Jack's place gave him an idea.

Freddy went straight to the bar to pick up Alice. Hurrying her along, he was no longer in the mood to drink. He had other things on his mind.

Jack, not knowing he was found out, cornered Katie.

"What do you think you are doing? Getting knocked up? I don't want another kid! Goddamn it!" Leaving Katie once again alone, he went back to the house. "What am I gonna do?" he asked himself, leaving the car where it was.

Maddy, seeing how distressed her husband was, asked, "Jack, what's wrong? Maybe I can help."

"You, help?' he laughed. "You've got to be kidding? You couldn't even help yourself eleven years ago."

She understood what he was saying.

"Oh, that poor child! Pregnant!" Maddy cried out.

Finally finding a bottle he had hidden, Jack grabbed it and headed outside to be alone and think. After taking a couple big drinks, he went back into the house and went straight to the bedroom, slamming the door behind him

Maddy just finished the dishes when she heard Jack come through the front door. Recognizing his mood, she did not say a word to him, only watched him enter their bedroom, shutting the door behind him.

"Baby girl, how would you like it if your momma sleeps with you tonight?"

"Yes, Mommy, that will be fun!" Jackie clapped her hands together.

Katie was still in shock. She wanted her mama! Sitting back on her bed, she rocked back and forth, tears covering her face.

After a rough, sleepless night, and realizing Jack was not coming that morning, she continued working at her window, making headway in a corner. She was able to get her finger into a hole and reach through toward the outside. Feeling successful, she jumped down from her chair. She had to find something bigger than her little nail to help her.

In all the confusion, Jack had forgotten to put back the shackle on her ankle, which made it easier for her to walk around more freely. Searching all over the room, she had to find something better than her nail.

Jack stayed away for days after finding out about the pregnancy. No visits also meant no food! Water—she could always get from the tiny sink. Even though Katie was extremely hungry, she did not care.

It also meant no sex and no pain! She had these few days to just relax and think.

Four days later the door was opened. Her devil was back, and her peace was over! The only good thing was the food. But what she had to do as repayment!

Jack set the food tray down and left. This was the first time he didn't stay. Relieved, Katie took the plate and began eating. She was starving! It was a long time since she got to eat by herself, and when they finished, Jack would always take the dishes and utensils away. This time he left them all behind: the plate, the cup, and the spoon. He had left a spoon! Taking the opportunity, she took it and hid it right away from him in case he came back to collect the dishes. It would be a much better tool than her nail to help in her digging around the window. Holding the spoon by the scoop, Katie was able to use the handle to dig into the putty around the window. Some more good news; Jack still forgot the chain was off.

He had lots on his mind. He needed to get the sheriff to look at Gordon again as a top suspect. When he dropped off the food for Katie, he took what was left of her torn blouse. This was what he would use to plant, somehow, on James Gordon. How this was to happen, he was not sure. But the plan suddenly just fell right into his lap.

While finalizing the details of his trip, Jim said he had to run one last time into town. It was the opening he needed.

Jack asked, "I'm pretty much done for the day, care if I tag along? The ole lady wants me to pick up a few things from the store."

"Sure, I'll buy you a beer," James offered, believing Jack was a friend.

"Great, let me get my wallet." While at the car, he picked up the blouse and stuffed it in his pocket. Climbing up into Jim's truck, Jack shouted out happily, "Let's get out of here."

The drive into town was quick and full of talk. Jim excitedly talked about his trip while Jack pretended to listen. He asked all the right questions to keep the man talking while he was thinking to himself how he was gonna make the drop.

Finding a parking spot in front of the O'Connor store, Jim said, "Do your shopping, Jack, and I'll meet you back here in an hour."

"Sounds good, see you in an hour," Jack said and walked up the sidewalk toward the grocery.

With her newly found tool, Katie excitedly worked away at the windowsill. The job was progressing remarkably quicker. As she dug more and more in the hole, it became larger and larger. Soon she was able to stick her whole finger in it. As she jumped down from the chair, hope filled her heart. Kissing her prized spoon, she went to put it back in its secret place.

Jack hurriedly ran into the local market and grabbed up the first items he came upon.

After paying for his items and heading back, he thought about stopping at his buddy's. He had not talked with Freddy since their argument but decided there wasn't time, so he just proceeded back to the O'Connor store.

Jack saw Jim and Joseph talking, standing out by Gordon's truck. As he hurried to the passenger side, he leaned across the seat and dropped the blouse onto the driver's floorboard. He slammed the door and went to join the men as they talked.

Jim acknowledged him, "Joseph, you know Jack Hayes? He's been doing some work for me at home."

"Yes, I know Jack," Joseph replied, not looking at him.

"Mr. O'Connor, I want to apologize for what I said a few weeks ago. I didn't mean anything," Jack said addressing him politely.

Ignoring him, Joseph turned and started to walk back into the store.

Just as Jim was about to step into his truck, he saw a piece of clothing on the floor.

"What's this?" he asked, picking up the soiled material. Joseph turned around and was about to ask his friend what he said, "Where'd you get that?" Rushing back to the cab of the truck, he grabbed the item out of his friend's hands. "This looks like Katie's top. I remember her wearing it on her last day." As he held the blouse close, he could see there were red splotches all over it.

"What is this doing in your truck?" Joseph asked, holding it up for all to see.

"I don't know. It's the first time I've seen that."

"You have a lot of explaining to do… You're coming with me," Joseph said, taking him by the arm and heading up the street toward the sheriff's department.

Jack just stood by the truck, smiling and saying to himself, "That's done!"

Dragging Gordon into the sheriff's office, "Dave, you here?" Joseph called out loudly.

The receptionist jumped up to stop them, "Hold on a minute! You can't just barge in here!" she called out.

Hearing the commotion, the sheriff came up to greet them.

"What's going on?" he asked before seeing Joseph with a tight hold on James Gordon. "June, I got this. Joseph, what the hell is wrong with you? Both of you come with me," he ordered the two men.

As he led the way into the conference room, the sheriff had both men take a seat.

"Now tell me what this is all about?"

Joseph jumped to his feet.

"This was found in his truck," he said, holding up the soiled material. "It was the top Katie was wearing the day she disappeared."

He handed the top to the sheriff.

Dave examined the piece of clothing, seeing that it was torn.

"You sure this is Katie's?" he asked, also noticing the red stains all over it.

"Sheriff, I know it's hers. Is that blood?"

"Don't jump to conclusions. I'll have to send it out for evaluation. it could take two to three weeks. Besides, you've known Jim for years. He saw Katie grow from a little girl to a young lady," the sheriff reminded Joseph.

"Yes, Joseph, you know I would never hurt your girl. I love her as if she was my own!" James confirmed what the sheriff had said.

"But still, Jim, it does look bad. I can't let you leave town until we get this figured out," the sheriff informed him.

"My trip! I was leaving this weekend."

"Sorry, I can't let you leave town until I get this resolved," the sheriff told him.

"Damn it, Dave, you know I have nothing to do with any of this!" James cried then turned his attention back to Joseph. "You too. I have nothing to do with Katie being missing. You done with me? I got things to do!" James said in anger when Joseph didn't reply.

"Jim, it's normal procedure," Dave said.

"Normal my ass! Dave, this is me!" James shouted as he stormed out the door, slamming it behind him.

"Joseph, I'll be in touch," the sheriff said as he walked him to the door and stopped at the receptionist desk. "June, get me the Santa Fe State Police Department. We have a problem!"

Jack was waiting at Gordon's truck. He saw anger on Jim's face and did not say a word, just climbed into the truck. The drive back to the house was quiet; the anger could be felt in the air.

"Jack, my plans just changed. I'll just have you finish what you're doing, and I'll get back with you later if I need anything else done."

"Sure, Jim, I'll keep in touch," Jack replied.

Joseph drove home quickly.

"Margaret!" he called out as he came in the front door. "Something has showed up! I found something of Katie's!"

Margaret rushed down the stairs, "What did you say about Katie, something was found?"

"Yes, darling, I found Katie's top in Jim Gordon's truck," he told Margaret. "In Jim's truck!" he said to himself in disbelief.

"What was Katie's top doing in Jim's truck? He's one of our dearest friends," Margaret said, holding her husband's hands.

"I don't know yet! Dave is going to send it out for evaluation due to what looks like blood on it." As soon as he said those words, he regretted it.

"Blood! There was blood on the top? Is it Katie's?"

"We'll have to wait and see if it is. Dave says it takes a few weeks. The blood might not even be hers… Just think, this is the first lead we've had since all this happened," Joseph said, hugging his wife.

Katie had not seen her captor in days. She had time to heal and get used to the fact she was having a baby. She tried to remember the last time she had her period, to figure how far along she was. Three, maybe four months ago! Deep in her thoughts, she did not hear the door open.

Happy with himself, Jack drove home. He had not seen Katie in days, so he went straight there and let himself inside.

"Baby, I've missed you, we have a lot of catching up to do. Come to Papa!"

He grabbed her arm and yanked her toward him. He then pushed her up against the wall and, as he unzipped, jammed himself into her and pounded away into her.

Screaming, Katie tried to get away, hitting him with her fists.

"No! Please stop! You're hurting me!" she cried out.

"Shut up, bitch! I'll stop when I'm ready to stop! I want to show you who is boss, and you will always do as I say! I did not say to have a baby. No, I did not forget!"

When he finished, he just threw her on the bed and walked out. He was blaming her for the pregnancy.

"He is sick!"

As he entered the house, Jack ordered his wife, "Fix me something to eat. *Now!*"

Maddy did not utter a word and just followed his orders when she saw the mood her husband was in. She learned early in their marriage when to keep her mouth shut.

Jack took a sandwich to Katie but did not stay; after he refilled her water jug, he just left.

CHAPTER 13

I Thought We Were Friends

Three weeks went by, and finally, the results came in on the blouse. A perfect match! It was Katie's blood on the material. The O'Connors had given her toothbrush to them to use for DNA.

The sheriff ordered two of his deputies, "Go out to the Gordon residence and bring James Gordon in. It looks like he has some explaining to do!" After the two left, he paged the front desk, "June, give Joseph a call and ask him and his wife to stop in."

"Will do, Sheriff," she replied and called their store, hoping to catch them there.

Joseph found his wife in the stockroom.

"Margaret, the sheriff wants to meet with us."

"Oh Joseph, do you think they found out something?" she asked her husband as they hurried out the door.

The sheriff was waiting for them in his office; June took them back as soon as they arrived.

"Thank you, June," Dave said as he pointed to a chair for Margaret to sit. Joseph stood behind her.

"Dave, do you have any news? It's been three weeks!" Joseph asked the sheriff.

"Yes, Joseph, Margaret. I did get the results back. It is…Katie's blood," he sadly told them.

"*No!*" Margaret screamed out then just cried in her hands.

Joseph put his arms around her shoulders.

"Are you sure?" he asked.

"Yes. Sorry to tell you, it was a perfect match! It is Katie's blood!"

"What does this mean? That Katie is dead?" Joseph asked while Margaret, unable to speak, kept crying.

"As to what you are asking, I don't know what it means. Yet!" the sheriff admitted. "My men are bringing James Gordon in at this very moment for questioning, and I have the state police coming back."

"That son of a bitch! I thought he was my friend!"

Jack just finished his work at the Gordons'. From what he had heard, all plans for his employer's trip were once again cancelled. This left Jim in a terrible mood. Jack stuck his head around the corner of the new office.

"Jim, I'm done for the day and getting ready to leave. Anything else you need done before I head out?"

"No, Jack, thanks for all your work," Jim said, dismissing him without looking up.

Jack turned and walked out to his car and proceeded to drive away. He had to pull over on the drive to allow a patrol car to pass. Stopping on the side of the road, he turned around in his seat to watch what was going on.

James heard a car pull up to the house and opened the garage door.

"What did you forget?" he asked, thinking it was Jack returning, but was surprised to see the deputies. "What can I do for you guys?"

"James Gordon, we need for you to come into town with us right now," one of the deputies insisted.

"What's this all about, Deputy?" he asked.

"The sheriff has a few questions for you, and we were told to bring you in right away."

Teresa, seeing the deputy's car, approached her husband, "Honey, what's going on?"

"Nothing you need to worry about. The sheriff just needs to talk to me."

"Does it have anything to do with your trip and why you had to cancel?"

"Yeah! I'll get everything all straightened out," he told her as he climbed into the deputy's car.

Jack watched Gordon get into the back seat of the patrol car. With a big smile on his face, he continued his drive home.

In town James was told to wait for the sheriff in his office. After retrieving the packaged evidence, the sheriff entered the room while the two deputies waited in the hall.

"Thanks for coming in," Dave said, greeting his friend.

"It didn't sound like I had a choice! What's going on?" Jim answered sarcastically.

"Well, it seems we have a problem!" Dave declared, throwing the package on the table in front of him.

"What kind of problem? That looks like the material that came out of my truck. What gives?" Jim asked, picking up the package and examining it.

"Yes, that is the piece of clothing that came out of your truck a three weeks ago. It came back having Katie's blood all over it. Can you explain why, and how, it got in your truck?" The sheriff wanted answers.

"Hell, I don't know! What are you saying?" James asked.

Through the window, he motioned for his men to enter the room.

"Jim, I'm sorry to say... You are under arrest! You have the right to remain silent... Anything you say can and will be used against you in a court of law... You have the right to an attorney..."

One of the officers proceeded to handcuff him.

"*What the hell! Are you arresting me?*"

"Yes, Jim, I'm afraid I am," the sheriff replied.

"I have no idea where that came from and how it got in my truck! I have nothing to do with Katie being missing! Dave, you know me, I would never do anything like that!"

"Sorry, Jim, you had better call your attorney," the sheriff advised him.

Feeling defeated, James said, "I need to call Dan Stewart."

The sheriff handed James the phone before escorting him to a jail cell. He then put in an order to pick up and impound the Gordon truck.

Teresa answered a knock at the door and found three officers waiting outside. One of the officers handed her a piece of paper.

"Ma'am, we have a warrant to search your house and grounds," the deputy told her as they entered the residence.

Stepping aside, she allowed them to enter. She just walked around to the back deck to sit and wait. She did not want to watch them searching the house, going through all their personal things. As she sat and waited, she held tightly onto the search warrant and had tears running down her face.

The men searched all through the house, not missing one room, making a mess as they threw out items out of closets. They went up in the attic; one of the deputies went down in the crawl space, searching. Finding nothing, they continued their search in the garage and outer buildings. Walking the grounds, the deputies concluded their search and went back to town.

Teresa went into the house and was devastated of what she found. The rooms were trashed by the officers in their search. She sat down in the first chair she came to and cried her heart out.

The next morning at work, Joseph heard of an arrest. In the morning paper, he saw a picture of James Gordon on the front page, arrested and the main suspect in the O'Connor case. Throwing the newspaper aside, he rushed toward the sheriff's department. Dave Thomas was expecting him.

"Joseph, let me explain what's going on. Nothing is definite, but we did make an arrest last night."

"Yes, I saw in the newspaper this morning. We have known him all our lives. He stood up with me at my wedding! Is it true? That Jim had something to do with Katie being missing? I know I saw that top come out of his truck, and I got so angry that day when I marched him in here, but I cannot believe he would do something like this. With our Katie!" Joseph was feeling confused. His best friend—the prime suspect in his missing daughter's case.

"I can't believe it either! We're still working it all out. His arraignment was this morning and allowed to bond out. He's not considered a flight risk. The preliminary hearing is not set yet. Now you, under no circumstances, go near him! I'd hate to lock you up too! Let us do our job! Do you understand? *Do you understand?*"

"Understand!"

Back at his store, Joseph informed his manager he was gonna be gone for a few hours, then he left for home to update Margaret with the news.

Seeing Joseph drive up, she greeted him at the door, "Joseph, it's all over the news… Jim has something to do with Katie?"

"Yes, that's what it looks like!"

"I've got to see Teresa! I've got to see what she knows about this."

Early the next morning Margaret left to drive out to the Gordon house. She had to see Teresa. Twenty minutes later, she arrived at the Gordons' residence. Before leaving her car, Margaret just sat, putting her thoughts together on how she was to approach her good friend.

Ringing the doorbell, she waited for several minutes. Finally, the door opened, and Margaret was soon facing her friend.

"Teresa, can we talk?"

Teresa, seeing who the visitor was, immediately shut the door.

"Go away," she said through the door.

"I just want to talk. Will you please open the door?"

"No, I have nothing to say to you! You think Jim has something to do with Katie? How could you even think such a thing! All our friends know Jim was arrested!"

"Teresa, honey, please let me in so we can talk. Please open the door."

Hearing the lock unlatch and the door open, Margaret entered the house and took her friend into her arms.

"Margaret you know Jimmy has nothing to do this. Right!" Teresa said, pleading.

"Teresa, I know! But we need to talk about this. Why *was* Katie's blouse in your husband's truck? I've got to know! There has to be a simple explanation!"

"I don't know! They arrested him! My Jimmy! Maybe for murder! Jimmy would not hurt a fly! Yes, he fishes, hunts a little too. You know how much he loves your little girl! We both do! I was just about to leave for town to pay his bond and bring him home. They impounded his truck also to look for any more evidence that can put her in the truck. The sheriff's deputies were here last night, searching the house. In the attic, under the house, and out in his garage. Everywhere! They tore up everything. To think Dave would believe Jimmy had anything to do with this. I am so…humiliated. I can never show my face in town ever again."

"But why, Teresa? Why was that found in your husband's truck? Where is Katie?" Margaret grabbed Teresa by the shoulders. "Where is my Katie? Is she still alive?"

"You still think my Jimmy has anything to do with this? Get out! Get out of my house now!"

Teresa pushed her out the front door and slammed it behind her.

Margaret got back in her car and just sat there.

CHAPTER 14

The Loss

Katie was feeling better and was working longer at her project. She dug more and more around the window and was soon able to grab hold of a whole corner. Holding onto her belly, she jumped down from the chair on which she was standing. Starting to show, anyone could see she was pregnant. Sitting on her bed, she took long drinks of water to quench her thirst. *How long has it been since I've had a coke?* she thought to herself. It had to be close to a year as she tried calculating in her head. She missed her birthday, her mom and dad's birthday... School! She was supposed to have started college. Libby and Lisa—did they go on to college and continue their lives? She hoped so. And Charlie! Was he dating again? She remembered back to that awful day they broke up, the terrible things he called her. Maybe she was a flirt? And that other name, a prick tease? Katie hung her head in shame; maybe this was why all this happened to her. She was flirting with danger, and that danger caught up with her, leaving her kidnapped and pregnant!

She wondered how all her friends, her parents, would feel now, knowing she was about to have a baby. To Libby, she had told all her deepest secrets, especially the one that she was still a virgin! Libby could not believe that she had not done the deed yet!

"Two years, Katie, and nothing! Gosh! Me and Danny... *Wow!*" Libby had said.

Constantly hungry, Katie could not get enough to eat. On occasion Jack would bring her lemon cookies. She loved those cookies and could not get enough of them.

After a week, Jack again began staying all night with Katie. Several times during the night she found herself roughly awakened by him. At times when he was on her, he would feel the roundness of her belly against him, and it reminded him of the *Problem*! Putting an end to his desire, he would push her away, off the bed, to the hard, cold ground. Lying there, she would try to sleep with no blanket or pillow, shivering in the night.

Waking the next morning, Jack would just step across her body, leaving her where she slept, and go help himself with breakfast.

Since James Gordon's arrest, Jack was no longer working. Hearing that Gordon had bonded out and was back home, he thought he might go out and pay his dear friend a visit.

After Teresa bonded her husband out of jail, things were not pleasant in their home. Teresa worried and was constantly questioning her husband.

"Hon, what are we going to do? How *did* that piece of clothing get in your truck? I've been driving over to Edgewood to do the shopping. I'm too embarrassed to go into town."

"I don't know how that got in my truck! The last time I saw Katie was that Wednesday before she disappeared on Friday. You know I have nothing to do with this! Right?"

"Yes, of course! Margaret came out to see me, and she was so upset! Not because Katie is still missing but because of you being a suspect! She is so confused and not even thinking straight!"

"I have Dan working on it. We just need to keep the faith! The truth will come out!" he said, hugging his wife. "Soon I can have my truck back. At least they didn't find anything else."

Teresa glared at him after hearing the statement he just said.

"What do you mean by that? At least they didn't find anything else!"

"You know what I meant. That just didn't come out right."

While sitting out back on the patio, they heard the doorbell.

"Now what?" Jim went to see who their caller was. Glancing out the front window, he saw Jack Hayes standing on the porch. "What does he want now?" Opening the door, he said, "Jack, what can I do for you? I know all your work is completed."

"Jim, I couldn't remember. I thought you said you had something else for me to do."

"No, sorry, Jack, everything else is put on hold. I'm sure you heard my trip was cancelled. I'll just call you when, and if, I need you."

"Sorry to hear that. Like I said, I don't get to hear much what goes on in town since I live so far out. Just get a note to me somehow. I don't have a phone. Don't believe in 'em," he said as they shook hands. He proceeded back to his car.

Jack, thinking out loud, said, "While I'm out, I might as well stop in to see Freddy. I need to see if he's heard anything else."

As he drove back to Albuquerque, he was thinking how he could get information out of Freddy without making him suspicious. Jack knocked loudly on the front door.

"Fred, you home?" he called. Finding it unlocked, he proceeded inside. "Freddy, where are you?" Jack called out again.

"Here I am," Freddy answered, coming out of the kitchen.

"I just want to apologize for the other day, the way I ran out on you. Like I said, I got a lot on my mind," Jack addressed his friend.

"Didn't you think I could help you with your little problem!"

"I know, but I've got to figure this out on my own," Jack insisted.

"Maybe I want in!" Freddy insisted.

"What are you talking about?" Jack asked, getting irritated.

"I said, I want in! Let me explain. I know what your little problem is!"

"What the fuck are you talking about?"

"That day you left the bar in such a hurry, well, I followed you home!"

"You did what?"

"Yeah! I saw her at your place!"

"*Saw who?*" Jack shouted, starting to break into a sweat.

"Your little problem! The town's missing girl! Kaitlyn O'Connor!" Freddy declared.

He was enjoying himself, making Jack sweat.

Rushing toward Freddy, Jack grabbed him around the throat and pushed him up against the wall.

"You saw nothing! You hear me? *Nothing!*"

Struggling to fight Jack off, Freddy was finally able to push him away.

"Hey, I'm not gonna say anything. I just want in! I hate Joseph O'Connor just about as much as you do! All the times he's called the law on me. I want a piece of the action!"

Jack walked to the closest chair and dropped down in it.

"*No!* She's mine! It has nothing to do with her daddy or his money! I just want her!"

"Look at all the money we can make! O'Connor will pay a fortune to get his little girl back!"

"Like I said, I am not out for the money!"

"Are you crazy or just plain stupid? What are you going to do when you're finished with her? Just let her go! Have you thought that far ahead yet? You think she not gonna talk? Man, *think*," Freddy said, hitting his finger against Jack's forehead.

Jack had not thought about that, what he was gonna do with her when he was finished in his fun. And now the other big problem—pregnant!

Seeing how his words shook his friend, Freddy knew he had found a way in.

"We might as well get some money out of it too. Here's what we do…"

"*No!*" Jack shouted, jumping out of the chair and grabbing his friend again around the throat. "I will handle this! In my own way!" he snarled, pushing Freddy into the door.

"Calm down!" Freddy called out, as he was starting to lose his ability to move. The look in Jack's eyes scared him. He thought to himself, *I might have just pushed Jack too far!*

Jack kept a tight grip around his throat, squeezing more and more and watching the life go out of his friend's eyes. Releasing his grip, Fred Gates slid down the wall and slumped to the floor.

"What have I done? I killed him!" Jack said, coming to his senses.

Thinking fast, he found an old blanket, laid it on the floor, and rolled the body onto it. He then wrapped the blanket around the body. As he was leaving the room, he saw a small .38 revolver laying on the bedroom dresser.

Taking it and shoving it in his back pocket, Jack spoke out loud, "He won't be needing that now!"

Stepping out on the back porch, he looked all around the backyard to see if anyone was around. Finding it clear, Jack dragged the body out the back door and placed it behind the trash cans, using other bags to cover him. Going back through the house and out the front door, he slowly walked toward his car. Glancing up and down the street and seeing no one, he got into his car and drove slowly out of town.

Halfway home, Jack pulled to the side of the road and turned off the engine. Needing to calm his nerves, he pulled a bottle of tequila out of the glove box. After taking a big swig, he set the bottle beside him on the seat. Holding his hands up in front of him, he examined them. They were shaking uncontrollably.

Speaking to himself out loud, Jack said, "What have I done? Freddy, why did you make me do this?" As he retraced his steps in his mind, Jack wondered, "Did I leave any evidence behind?"

Calming himself, he remembered he was always at Freddy's. His prints would be all over that house! After emptying the bottle, he tossed it out the window and continued his drive.

Remembering what Freddy had said about the afterward got him thinking. What *was* he gonna do with Katie afterward? He couldn't let her just walk away. Sell her? Kill her? What about the baby she was carrying? It had to be dealt with immediately!

Entering the room, Jack found Katie fast asleep on her bed.

"Hey, girlie, playtime!" Katie woke but did not get a chance to sit up before she was dragged off the bed. "Why did you have to ruin everything and get pregnant? Don't you women know anything? Madeline! And now you!" he shouted and threw her against the wall. "I have never wanted a baby! Not then or again now!"

Picking her up off the ground, he slammed his fist into her stomach and then let her fall again to the hard ground. Giving her a couple swift kicks to her stomach with his boots, Jack left her there.

Immediately the pain started. Picking herself off the ground, Katie crawled to her bed. Sitting on the floor, her back pressed up against the bed, she knew something was wrong.

She cried out as the pain increased. She quickly realized what was happening; she was losing her unborn child. Fearing the danger, she started praying. Would she survive, or did she really want to? Feeling pressure, she knew the baby was coming very quickly. Leaning back against her bed and bringing her knees up toward her, she screamed out loud, and the child expelled from her womb. Needing something to cut the umbilical cord, she remembered her spoon. Hoping it would work, she took her spoon and sawed on the cord until she separated it from the child. Thinking that she was around four months pregnant, she knew it had no chance. She saw that her baby was a little girl and that it had not survived. After ridding herself of the afterbirth, she wrapped the baby in her blanket and gently laid her upon the bed. Walking slowly to her sink, she took a cloth, and after rinsing it in cold water, she laid beside her baby on the bed. Holding the cold cloth against her, she hoped it would help ease up the bleeding. When it looked like the bleeding was under control, Katie took her daughter in her arms, laid back, and slept the night away.

Waking early the next morning, Katie knew she had to find a way to bury her child. Still in pain, due to both the beating and the birth of her child, she knew she had to hurry before Jack reappeared. Finding an old crate to place her baby in, Katie gave her a final kiss and covered her with old, dirty potato sacks. Taking her to a far-back corner in the room, she made a little grave. As much as she despised the baby's father, this was her baby girl.

"Rest in peace, my little one!"

Cleaning her bed and washing the blankets in cold water, she then laid them close to the heater to dry. Her body was filthy from dried blood. She was worried about infection.

Katie was slow to get back on her feet. It was two weeks before she was able to continue working on her project. She moved slowly and was unable to work for more than fifteen minutes at a time. The good part was that Jack stayed away for over a week. But that also meant no food. Jackie still came to visit, and Katie tried to hide the pain she was in from her. Jackie, not knowing Katie was pregnant, saw a difference in her friend, how she was slowly moving around. She asked often what was wrong.

Katie just told her she fell off her chair and bruised a rib. That seemed to satisfy the girl's curiosity.

Finally, on the seventh day, Jack appeared, bringing food.

Seeing the mess in the bucket, he smiled and said, "I see that problem has been taken care of!"

CHAPTER 15

Murder

The state police arrived back in town the following week. With the door shut to his office, the sheriff filled the lieutenant in on what had aspired.

Handing over the envelope containing the soiled blouse, he said, "Here's what was found." Then he continued, "Actually, it was found in the truck of one of the people we interviewed. James Gordon!"

As the trooper opened the file, he read over the interview.

"Yes, I see where we talked with him ourselves. A close friend of the family! They usually are the last people we suspect."

"I just don't see it! He does a lot for the community. A model citizen! He was just as shocked seeing that piece of clothing as we were. I believe him!" the sheriff added.

"Well, he could just be shocked 'cause he messed up by forgetting about it being in his truck. You said you thoroughly checked his house, the garage? The whole premises? Could he be holding her somewhere else?" All these questions were asked as the lieutenant reread the report.

"My officers walked his whole property. I'll check to see if there are any other places where he could have her hidden. He was getting ready to go out on his yearly fishing trip. Of course, I cancelled that. I'll run up and have a talk to the manager at the registration office of the cabin he was going to stay at and see if he happened to check in early or has another place booked," the sheriff informed the lieutenant.

"Good idea! You said this Gordon made bail? When is his preliminary hearing?"

"Yes, he's not going anywhere. His hearing is in three weeks, April 4."

Joseph O'Connor went on with his daily business. He was still unable to understand how his good friend could have anything to do with his missing daughter. But he saw with his own eyes the piece of Katie's clothing in Gordon's truck. Knowing the hearing was the first week in April, he was planning to sit up front, facing who he thought was his good friend.

Jack no longer had any access to the Gordons. He was hoping to plant more evidence inside the office he built but had no chance to get there. Also, the truck Gordon just got out of impound was safely locked away in his garage. He had to get in that garage!

There was an awful smell in town, and people were calling the sheriff office for over a week.

"Goddamn it!" Sheriff Thomas said, getting irritated. "I don't have time for this." He sent a deputy out to investigate. The smell was coming from the vicinity of Fred Gates's house. "Of course, who else!" he added.

The deputy knocked on the front door of the Gates residence. The smell was horrible! Receiving no answer, he then pounded on it.

"Sheriff's Office!" Still no answer. Finding the door unlocked, he slowly entered the house. "Mr. Gates, you home? Sheriff's Office!" Checking out each room, the kitchen was last, of which he entered with caution. The smell was dreadful throughout the whole house. But it was stronger and getting worse as he walked through the kitchen toward the back door. "Must be a dead dog or something," he said to himself. Walking down the back steps, he headed toward the trash cans. "That damn Gates must have killed the neighbor dog and threw the body in one of the trash cans."

Sifting through the bags of trash while holding his breath, the stench was *so strong!* Seeing what looked like an old blanket and finding an opening, he moved away some of the material. The deputy found not the body of a dog but the body of Fred Gates!

Stumbling out from among the trash and toward the back porch, the deputy lost what was in his stomach. On his radio, he called the sheriff.

"Sheriff, you better get over here to the Gates's house!"

Hearing the radio calling his name, the sheriff picked it up, "What did he do now?"

"What he did was go and get himself killed!" the deputy stuttered.

"*What!*" The sheriff grabbed his hat, stopping at the front desk. "June, clear my day and get ahold of the coroner. Give him Fred Gates's address and have him meet me there."

"Yes, sir," she answered, picking up the phone.

The closer he got to Gates's house, the stronger the smell.

Finding his deputy on the front porch, the sheriff confronted him, "You sure it's Gates?"

"I'm pretty sure, Sheriff, but there is a lot of decomposing. It does resemble him. I tell you, this is the first time I've seen a dead body. Sure, in the academy, I saw cadavers, but not like this at an actual crime scene! Sorry, sir," he said, running to the other side of the porch to throw up again.

"Not mine!" the sheriff replied back. "It has been a while though! Where's the body? We need to tape this off," he said, pointing out the whole backyard.

"It's around back, just off the back porch," the deputy said, wiping his mouth as he led the way around the house.

Coming upon the body, the sheriff asked, "You touch anything around the body?"

"Sir, I only moved aside some of the blanket he's wrapped in and take some trash bags off the body to get a better look."

"Good!"

Two hours later, the coroner announced himself.

Kneeling, he also asked, "You touch anything?"

The sheriff answered, "No, my deputy told me what little he disturbed, which was only some trash and a corner of the blanket." More of his deputies had arrived and began to tape off around the house and bagging all items that surrounded the body, even the branches and leaves, anything could tell the story of what happened.

The coroner had two of the deputies pull the body out from the trash cans and helped put it in the body bag. In doing this, the sheriff saw the bruising around Freddy's throat.

As they walked through the house, the sheriff noticed a stain running down one wall just outside the kitchen. After a close examination, it smelled like urine.

As he watched them finish bagging the body and carry it to the examiner's car, he asked the coroner, "How do you think he died?"

"I saw some bruising around his throat. I have a feeling strangulation might be the case. Once I get him back to my office, I can do a thorough exam."

"I saw the bruises too. Something must have happened in here," Dave said, pointing out a turned-over chair, a lamp knocked to the floor, and magazines scattered all over the living room. "Unless he took a piss on that wall," Dave added, pointing to the doorway of the kitchen, "it happened there. I bet he was then dragged outside."

The coroner agreed, "You're probably right! Once I do the autopsy, I'll get you the full report."

The sheriff walked the coroner out of the house and toward his car to drive back to Santa Fe. He had a job to do.

The state police heard about the murder in town. The lieutenant went in search of the sheriff and found him in his office.

As he stepped inside, he asked, "You think this has anything to do with the missing girl?"

"We don't know yet. He was the first person we interviewed, living directly across from the store. He said he didn't see anything. Fred Gates was just the town drunk," the sheriff answered.

"We talked with him also and didn't get much out of him either. But now with his murder, did Mr. Gates know more than he let on? Maybe, just maybe, he saw who took the girl, and when the perpetrator found this out, he had to take him out of the equation. That... or...our Mr. Gates confronted him, wanting hush money," the lieutenant said, making a guess.

"That does sound like something Freddy would do. I was just getting ready to go out and question Jack Hayes, his drinking buddy. They were like two peas in a pod!" Sheriff Thomas informed him of his plans.

At that moment the door opened, and Alice Cook, running through the door, almost collided with the sheriff.

Tears in her eyes, she asked, "Sheriff, is it true? About Freddy? Is he really dead?"

"Yes, Alice, I'm very sorry, but it is true! We're in the middle of the investigation. I'm glad you're here. It saves me the trouble of rounding you up. Come in, we need to talk. This is Lieutenant Reynolds, he'll be joining us," Dave said as he led her to an empty room.

The trooper tipped his hat, "Ma'am."

"Like I said, I'm sorry you had to find out about his death this way. I would have liked to have told you myself. I know how close you and Freddy were," the sheriff said in a gentle voice as he pulled out a chair for her to sit.

"Yes, I've stayed at his house a few times. We was talking marriage. Can you imagine me getting married? Me, the town floozie? I loved Freddy! He wasn't much, but he was mine!"

"Was he in any kind of trouble? Did he owe anyone money?" the lieutenant asked.

"No! None of that! If he didn't have the money to buy something, he would just wait to buy it when he did have cash. Just the other day he told me he was coming into some money. That's when we were gonna get married and move away. Far away from here."

The sheriff and lieutenant looked at each other.

The lieutenant continued his questions, "Did he happen to say where the money was coming from? Or when?"

"No! He said to be ready at a day's notice! I'm all packed, was just waiting for that call!"

"Alice, don't leave town in case we have more questions," she was told by both men.

As she was preparing to leave, Alice cried out, "*Oh my god!* Does Jack know yet?"

The sheriff answered, "I was just about to head that way when you came in."

"He will be so upset! He and Freddy were so close! Except that time a few weeks ago when they got into that huge argument at the saloon."

"What kind of argument?" both officers asked at the same time.

"Oh, just some stuff Jack said he was going through. I couldn't hear much, only Freddy offering to help and Jack getting mad. Jack cursed at him then fired out of there like a loose cannon. Freddy followed him and came back later. I never heard any more about it."

"It's a good thing you weren't at Freddy's when this happened. You could be laying on the slab alongside him. Take care now. I'll be in touch," Dave said.

Alice was led out by both men.

"You get all that? What she was talking about...the money?" the lieutenant asked the sheriff.

"Yep! First, I'm going out to Hayeses to see what that argument was about!"

"I'm coming with you," Reynolds said and joined him in the car.

Jack saw a car coming down the drive. As he waited on the porch, he saw it was from the sheriff department.

"What now?" Jack asked himself then quickly realized Fred's body was probably found. Even before the car had come to a complete stop, he yelled out to the men, "What do I owe the pleasure of your visit today?"

"Jack, this is Lieutenant Reynolds of the state police," the sheriff introduced the state trooper. "When did you last see your buddy, Gates?"

"Heard you guys were in town. Can't rightly say when I saw him last, probably a couple weeks ago. Why?"

"We found him dead today at his house."

"What? Freddy, dead? What the fuck happened?" Jack asked, acting shocked.

"Looks like he was strangled. I'll get all the details later today. What was that argument about, the one between you and Freddy a few weeks ago at the bar?" the sheriff continued with his questions.

"Oh, that? It was nothing! Just a misunderstanding!"

"Misunderstanding about what?" the sheriff asked, not giving up.

"What's this all about? You think I killed my best friend?"

"No! I'm just trying to get all the facts!" the sheriff informed him.

"Don't you have anything better to do besides harassing me?" Jack shouted at the men. "If you hear a gunshot, who is the first person you visit, me or Freddy? Well, I guess now since Freddy is gone… it's gonna be me all the time! Get off my land unless you have some kind of warrant!"

Seeing he was getting nowhere, Dave finished with, "We'll be in touch!" Both officers climbed back in the patrol car and drove off.

Joseph saw all kinds of activity going on across the street. He stepped out the door and walked toward the flashing lights. He had also complained of the bad smell that was all over the area. He thought it was probably a sewer problem. He saw the Gates house was all staked off with crime-scene tape, and approached one of the officers.

"Officer, what's going on?"

The deputy recognized Joseph O'Connor and told him the news, "It looks like Gates was killed!"

"Killed? When?" Joseph asked, shocked.

"We don't have the exact time of death, but it looks to be a strangulation. Don't quote me on that, the coroner has the body."

"My daughter missing! A murder! What is going on? Albuquerque used to be a quiet town. Do you think they have anything to do with each other?" Joseph wanted to know.

"I don't have any idea. That question should be addressed to the sheriff," the deputy answered.

"That I will do!" Joseph assured the deputy.

Maddy noticed Jack was much calmer, not as agitated. She wondered how Katie was doing and suspected that she might be pregnant. Maddy was worried about the poor girl's health and her having to deal with this issue all alone. She knew Katie would be frightened, and she would have loved to be with her but was afraid of Jack finding out. And somehow he always did. Jack knew everything that went on in the house. It's like he had cameras planted all through the house, inside and out. All she could do was make sure Katie had plenty to eat.

Maddy knew something was wrong when she noticed Jack was no longer going to work.

"He probably got himself fired!" she said to herself.

She asked on different occasions when he was leaving, and he would just shout out, "Mind your own business."

She just began to give all her attention to her daughter. After learning about the problems in school, she decided to just concentrate on Jackie and no one else. The school year was soon to end, and Maddy hoped her daughter had not fallen too far behind in her studies.

Katie regained her strength slowly and began to work feverishly on her project. With more confidence, she knew she would succeed and escape. In the mornings when she woke after Jack left and in the evenings before he came home, she would sit by the little grave that held her daughter, wiping away her tears before she walked away.

Jack still had not remembered the chain was off her ankle. She was relieved to be able to walk around freely without dragging that chain. She could get closer to the door now, but there was no way to open it.

Jack still stayed the night even though he was unable to "make love to his darling" during her cycle. Instead, he made her do things for him. It was more ways to humiliate her. Drawing her close to him as he slept, he had no idea, or did not care, of her loss. He was just glad the *problem* was gone! Things were almost back to normal in Jack Hayes's mind. He just had to decide what to do when his fun was over with Kaitlyn O'Connor! Since Freddy brought that issue to his attention, it made him realize, "What *am* I gonna do when I'm through with her?"

The sheriff department searched Fred Gates's house and property, looking for any clues. They knew where it happened but nothing telling them why. Nothing! Dave threw the file across the room.

"*Goddamn it!* First the O'Connor girl goes missing, now the murder of Fred Gates! Are they somehow linked?"

Dave Thomas has been in law enforcement for over twenty years, having solved hundreds of cases. Until now! When it involved one of his own good friends!

The coroner had finished the autopsy in record time and determined strangulation was the cause of death, as he stated in his report. The sheriff did his part and concluded that Gates was killed in his house and, finding that urine on the wall and carpet, knew where it happened. The overturned furniture told him there was a struggle. But with who? The officers all wanted to know.

CHAPTER 16

The Trial

The day finally arrived! April 4! As promised, Joseph O'Connor and his wife sat in the front row in the courtroom.

The prosecutor did his best to show now James Gordon was guilty. Everything he presented was objected to Dan Stewart, James's attorney. The sheriff had contacted the cabins Gordon could have stayed in all his trips, but that led to nothing out of the ordinary. In the end, all charges were dropped due to lack of evidence. Teresa Gordon hugged her husband while Margaret O'Connor cricd out.

The O'Connors were both relieved and upset. They were relieved that their good friend was apparently not involved and upset that they were back to square one.

Margaret joined Teresa in the doorway, saying, "I am so sorry you had to go through this! In my heart I knew Jim had nothing to do with it. Can you forgive me?"

"I'm not sure! The whole town thought Jim was guilty! I know what you are going through. Really, I do! I can imagine if any of my children came up missing, I'd probably act the same way. Give me time!"

Joining her husband, the Gordons left the courthouse.

Jack Hayes was sitting in a far-back corner of the courtroom. A person would never have recognized him, all cleaned up, hair combed, and wearing an old suit. He had watched the proceedings, full of anger! Nothing had gone the way he had hoped. Not enough evidence! Prominent citizen! Blah blah blah! He had to start looking in another direction to lead the police. A thought came to him, maybe good ole Freddy can finally help him! He slipped out a side door, hoping he wasn't noticed. He didn't want to cause the town to wonder why he was there.

With the trial over, the sheriff could again concentrate on the murder. Still, in the back of his mind, he thought, *Could these two cases be somehow linked?* The state police did what they could by stopping in at the saloon.

Lieutenant Reynolds entered through the door.

"Is the owner in?" he asked.

Finishing his job wiping off the counter, the bartender tossed the towel across his shoulder and introduced himself, "That's me, Hank Andrews, owner of this hole-in-the-wall bar." He shook the trooper's hand. "What can I do for you? I go by the books…serve no one under the age of twenty-one!"

"No, we're not here for that!" the lieutenant went on to say. "I'm sure you heard about Fred Gates being murdered?"

"Yes, my customers are all free in their talk in here. I get all the latest news. I know Freddy. He is one of my best customers…or should I say, was…" Hank answered soberly.

"What we do want to find out was about that argument he had with Jack Hayes about three weeks ago. Did you happen to hear anything? What it was about?" the lieutenant asked.

"Sorry, I just got the tail end of it, with Jack jumping up, yelling something at Freddy, then storming out of here. I heard nothing of how it started. Freddy ran off after him, leaving his date here alone."

"Yeah, Alice Cook was with him that day. We already got her story. She said, soon as Freddy got back, he paid their bill and left. How was Fred acting? Normal?"

"Now that you mention it, he did not act like himself. Like something was bothering him," Hank remembered.

The sheriff and the lieutenant now wanted to know what that argument was about. Jack Hayes was not saying anything, and they didn't feel like they had the grounds to bring him in.

With the trial behind them, Jim and Teresa decided to go away. Instead of him going on his trip with his buddies, this time Jim took with him his two beauties: his wife, Teresa, and the blue sapphire! In the weeks they were gone, Teresa began to understand why her husband enjoyed fishing so much. It was so relaxing! So peaceful! She would no longer dread his fishing trips because she would be joining him. She dressed in her finest: overalls, chest waders, and a big, floppy hat. She was set! Jim smiled, thinking to himself, *She is so beautiful!*

The deputies kept going back to the Gates house. Every room, every closet was searched over and over, in the attic and down in the crawl space. Still nothing surfaced! Again, a mystery! They took all kinds of fingerprints from door facings, windows, and doorknobs to be evaluated. They hoped to find something!

Jack again had to find work. With the Gordons gone, there was no chance of finding work there. His plan now was to use Freddy as his scapegoat. *As they say, dead men can't talk!* Jack thought. Freddy was not around to clear himself. The perfect solution! He needed to sneak into the house and find some place to plant evidence. Boom! The deed would be done! It had to be taken care of soon while the officers were still working the house. He had to go home and retrieve something else of Katie's.

Smiling to himself, he said, "I might as well get a little afternoon delight if she stopped her woman's curse."

He hated it when that happened, but not having anything for weeks was worse, so he was ready for some action.

Katie saw the door open.

Pushing her down upon the bed, Jack ripped off her panties and threw them to the ground. He made his demands. Katie screaming and hitting at him excited him more and made him plunge into her violently.

"Back to normal!"

Jack grinned and patted her on the behind. Before leaving, he grabbed her panties off the floor.

Katie had never experienced pain like this; losing her virginity had not been this bad. It felt like Jack was tearing her apart.

Parking at the saloon, Jack went in to have a drink. He not been back since his argument with Freddy. Taking a seat at his usual spot, the bartender immediately recognized him.

"I haven't seen you in a while!" he said as he placed a beer in front of him. "Sorry about what happened to your buddy."

"Yeah!" Jack replied quickly without compassion.

"A state trooper stopped by, asking questions about you," the bartender continued.

"What was he asking about?"

"Something about an argument between the two of you."

"What you say?"

"Nothing. I didn't hear anything of the conversation between you guys," he replied.

"Good! It was none of your business anyway," he said and threw a couple dollars at him and left.

The bartender noticed the change of attitude in Jack Hayes. It seemed like Jack couldn't care less about his buddy's death. He just shook his head and went on with his business.

Jack spoke to himself, "Freddy, even dead, you can still cause me trouble. I'll show you."

Thinking about it made him more obsessed with continuing with his plan. He saw no one when he got to Freddy's. He went around back and crawled through a window. The cops must have left it unlocked.

Taking the panties out of his pocket, he spoke out loud, "Where to plant them?" Finding a loose floorboard in one of the closets, he decided it was the perfect spot. Before replacing the board, he made sure some of the material was sticking out. "That will show you, you bastard!" he said to Freddy out loud.

Crawling back out the same window, he left the residence unseen, or so he thought!

"There has got to be something in that house! Go back through that house and tear out every board if necessary! *There has to be something there!*" the sheriff raised his voice.

He was so aggravated, always coming up with nothing! Joined in the search with his men, they walked through the house, stomping hard on the floor in all the rooms. Finally, in one of the closets, the sheriff came across a loose board with a piece of material sticking out. Kneeling, he pried up the board and found a piece of clothing.

"Guys, I thought I told you to look in all the closets?" Taking his pen, he pulled the material out between the boards, revealing a pair of panties. "Look what I just found!" Excited, he held the item up to show his men. Dropping them in a plastic bag, "Get these to the lab ASAP!" the sheriff shouted out.

"Sheriff, that was not there before, I swear to god! We checked all through the closets, finding nothing! We would have seen that!" a deputy responded, flabbergasted, thinking how they could have missed that.

Jack was in town the following week, trying to get news. While hanging out at his normal drinking hole, he heard about an update in the Gates case. The bartender said something was found in the house, Jack heard him say to a person who was sitting down from him at the bar. As he eased in, trying to listen in, he heard only the end of the conversation, which was nothing. He did hear that the bar was needing help. Bartending! He never thought about it, but it would be perfect! How hard can it be, mixing drinks and listening to everyone's problems, getting all the gossip around town!

"Who do I need to talk to about the job opening?" he asked the bartender.

"Me. I'm the bartender/dishwasher. They also call me the owner. I don't know, man! You? Serving drinks? Hell, you're one of my best customers!" He laughed. "You know you can't drink on the job, right?"

"Shit! I know that! I think I can survive through a day without drinking! How about it?" Jack asked, trying to convince the man.

"Okay, let's see how you do! I'll give you a trial run. By the way, my name's Hank."

"Great! Hank, when can I start?"

"How about tomorrow night? I'll show you the ropes. You're looking at evenings, 7:00 p.m. to 1:00 a.m. Weekends could be longer. Just remember, if I catch you drinking on the job, I'll fire your ass right on the spot! And another thing…clean yourself up!"

"Gotcha! No problem!" Jack beamed, shaking his boss's hand.

Jack's days turned into nights, and his nights into days. This also changed the Hayes household schedule, although Maddy and Jackie had no problem with it. Jack was very seldom in the house anyway, except to collect his meals and an occasional change of clothing. Katie's life was the one that changed the most. Jack sleeping all day disrupted her routine; she had to change her schedule too—from days to nights. He made her sleep when he slept. At least now she knew Jack wouldn't just show up at any time. He had set hours, and she soon learned that schedule and made it work for her. She was now working at night on her window and had a difficult time due to the limited light.

The results from the clothing found at the murder scene turned out to be excellent news. Katie's blood was found on them, along with semen. The only bad thing was that the semen did not match Fred Gates. The department ran the newly found information through their database, the results coming back, of course, no match!

As they were putting the pieces together, it seemed Mr. Freddy Gates was somewhat involved in Katie's case, with another accomplice! The worry the sheriff had now was, was Katie still alive? And if so, where was she? The sheriff decided to keep this newly found information under wraps until they could find the owner of the semen. He ordered all officers to not let the news leave the precinct under any circumstances.

In their morning meeting, the sheriff gave orders to his men, "Men, we are going to backtrack Gates's every move. Starting from last July. I want to see who he had contact with, worked with, or talked to. Even who he took a piss with! Visit the grocery and liquor store! Bring Alice back in. We need to get deep in her head and see if she heard anything or saw anything, even if she thought it was nothing. I feel we are getting somewhere now! *Get me something!*"

The sheriff demanded and then dismissed his men.

CHAPTER 17

The Bar

Jack found the job of his dreams and was getting paid as he did it. Along with it, a bonus: tips. The only downfall was working nights. He hoped he could get on days soon as he proved himself. Hank noticed right away what an asset Jack Hayes had become. He knew everyone in town and had a way of getting them to spend their hard-earned money. On occasion he would hand out free shots. Hank saw this but overlooked it because it made the customer buy even more. When he received his first paycheck, Jack informed Hank that he owed for some shots that he had given to a few of his friends. Jack, coming forward and telling him this, made Hank feel good about hiring him.

"No, Jack, that's okay! You're doing a great job!"

Maddy was happy in the new living arrangement with Jack working at night. Of course, she had to rearrange cooking the meals for him. He had a regular paycheck coming in, which meant he was able to keep food in the house. Jackie didn't get to see much of her daddy, but that didn't bother her. She hated being around him anyway. All she cared about was her mommy. She was doing much better in her studies at school, but she still kept to herself on the playground. The only person she allowed to become a close friend to her was Katie. They enjoyed being together and having long talks through the door.

Alice was brought back in the office for more questioning. She was not told about the piece of clothing that was found.

"Why all these questions about Freddy? He was killed! Find his killer!"

"Alice, we are! That's why all the questions. We need to know his last steps and who he last saw. These answers can lead us to his killer, and why! Anything can help! A phone call that sounded strange! An argument? Alice, think!" the sheriff drilled her.

"That day of the fight when Freddy came back from following Jack, he was acting really strange," Alice said, remembering that day.

"What do you mean by strange?" Sheriff Thomas asked her.

"We didn't stay much longer at the bar after he returned. I was talking to him on the way back to his place, and he wasn't even paying any attention to anything I said. I had to repeat myself several times! It was like he had something on his mind! When we got back to his place, he told me to go on home. I was puzzled about that 'cause he always wanted me to spend the night with him. A couple days later is when he told me about the money! And that we was getting married!"

"You said it was just after that argument when Fred chased after Hayes? How did you know he followed him?"

"He told me. He said he was worried about the state of mind Jack was in and wanted to make sure he got home all right."

"See, all this helps! You think of anything else, please don't hesitate to come in. Anything can help us make the pieces fit," the sheriff said and thanked her for coming in.

Alice, as she was preparing to leave, added, "I want to help all I can in finding my Freddy's murderer!"

The sheriff looked through all the notes he and the state police collected. He learned that the bartender said roughly the same thing about Freddy's quick departure and change of attitude.

Joseph could not understand why all communication from the sheriff had stopped. Dave at first was updating him weekly on any changes. Now? Nothing! Yes, there was a murder in town, but he selfishly thought, *He's dead, and my little girl could still be alive!*

The Gordons arrived home from their four-week trip. Their first stop was at the grocery before heading for home. They were updated on what all had happened while they were gone, especially the news on the murder of Fred Gates!

I've got to see Margaret and see if there is any news on Katie! Teresa thought as she entered through the store's doors and found her quickly.

Taking her hands in hers, she asked, "Margaret, have you heard anything new? Please tell me she's home!"

"Teresa, dear, nothing has changed! She is still missing! We've not heard anything for weeks!"

"We will pray! I am here for you!" Teresa cried, pulling her friend close.

Katie could not work on the window as much these days due to Jack. When he slept, she also had to sleep. He kept her close to him the whole day until it was time for him to leave for work at seven o'clock in the evening. Jack still did not notice the shackle was off, and Katie kept her leg hidden under the blanket so he would not be reminded. She ran the chain across the floor toward the bed to make him think all was okay.

Jack, having so much on his mind, did not even think about the chain. It was never in the way in their lovemaking.

Jack was earning so much respect from Hank from all his good work. The bar was making more money due to him. His changes in the evenings brought in more and more people. He talked Hank into adding pool tables and dart boards, which allowed customers to have tournaments and drink. He sold buckets of beer at a special price and served popcorn and pretzels. These salty items made his customers thirsty, which made them buy more.

One afternoon, before starting his shift, Hank called Jack into his office.

"Jack, I am very pleased with all your hard work. You've proved yourself to me and become a great asset. The changes you convinced me to make were all moneymakers. You almost doubled the profit coming in. I think you have found your calling. Congratulations!"

"Thank you, Hank. I really enjoy working here. It's just the late shift that sucks!"

"Well, I have good news for you! I am switching you to days. The excellent work you did on nights, I hope you can do the same on days!"

"That's great! My wife will be so pleased! I've got a lot of ideas already for you."

"Well, let's hear 'em!" Hank said, pulling up a chair and putting their heads together as they discussed the new plans.

Jack was starting to feel more at home there than at home itself. He always liked being in charge and getting that huge raise, and the day shift put him on top of the world. It was time for a celebration. He bought some champagne and strawberries and wanted to share his joy with his lady.

Juggling the items in his hands while opening the door, he said, "Baby, it is time for celebrating! I've been promoted to days." He picked her up in his arms and swung her around. "I brought champagne," he said, dangling the bottle in front of her, "and strawberries." He shoved the carton under her nose.

Katie took the strawberries and threw them at him.

"*You bitch!* Here I am, trying to be nice, and what do you do? Throw it in my face!" he shouted, shoving her.

"Nice? You call this nice?" she asked, gesturing at her surroundings. "I want to go home!" Katie cried out to him once more.

"Not until I am through with you! And I'm not done with you yet!" Jack replied.

CHAPTER 18

Witness

The murder case of Fred Gates was slowly coming together. The sheriff was beginning to figure out what might have happened. In their investigating, he did find out that Freddy was heavy into drugs—*coke!* A tiny amount of a white substance was found in a corner on the bathroom vanity. They bagged the powder, thinking it was baby powder, but found out later it was not. This was beginning to look like drugs might have been involved, so Dave made a call to the coroner.

"Did you by any chance do any blood tests and see if drugs were in Gates's system?" the sheriff asked.

"Let me bring up that report," the coroner said, pausing. "Yes, I did do a complete blood analysis, and it showed traces of cocaine in his bloodstream!" the coroner verified.

"And you failed to mention this?" Anger rose in the sheriff's voice.

"It's all in the report!" the coroner fired back.

"Sorry, Doc, thanks for your help," Dave said, hanging up the phone. "This has to be a drug exchange gone bad! But the big question is, how was Katie involved?"

Working on days, Jack was able to hear more news from the sheriff department. It was true that the more people drank, the more they talked. He heard a couple of deputies talking among themselves about the murder and, by moving closer and making believe he was wiping the counter, listened in.

"Yep, that old coot, I figured he was on something. He looked to be drunk all the time but was high instead," one of the deputies stated. "Now we have to track down his dealer."

Hearing this, Jack thought.

"Damn it, Freddy! I should have known you were into something! You better not mess up my plans!" Jack mumbled to himself as he cleaned.

All systems were now a go for Katie to continue her plan of escape. Jack was back on days, which helped her forge ahead with her project. She was getting closer and closer to the final stages of removing the window. All her patience was paying off, and she could just visualize the whole nightmare becoming her past.

Joseph O'Connor had not gotten any information for weeks on his daughter's case. He decided that he had waited long enough and called for the sheriff.

"Can I speak to the sheriff please?" he asked the receptionist.

After holding for a few minutes, the sheriff finally picked up.

"Joseph, I am really sorry that I have not gotten back with you in a while. I have not forgotten you. I'm just working out some details. Why don't you come in, say, in an hour? I will fill you in on what we've found so far. Come alone so we can keep this between us."

"You found something? Why haven't you told me, and why can I not bring Margaret?"

"Just come alone. You can decide what you want to tell her after," the sheriff insisted then hung up.

"What do you mean, what I want to tell her?" Joseph asked but realized the sheriff had already hung up.

Exactly one hour later, Joseph was facing Sheriff Thomas.

"What have you found out and don't have the decency to tell me?"

"Now, Joseph, don't get upset, but in Fred Gates's house, we found another piece of clothing that belongs to Katie!"

"And you felt I didn't need to know about this piece of information?"

"Hold on, there's more! It had blood on it like the top, but this time it also had semen on it."

Turning pale, Joseph leaned back in his chair. In his thoughts, *What kind of horror is my daughter going through?* He kept repeating it to himself over and over.

"That is why I felt only you should hear this piece of information. It's up to you what part of this conversation you want Margaret to know!" the sheriff explained.

"My poor girl! How is she surviving through this? Dave, what was her clothing doing at Gates's house?"

"You keep thinking survive! That means that she is still alive! Bits and pieces are surfacing like I said they would. We will find her! We're looking into what Gates has to do with Katie and why that piece of clothing was there. Now, this goes no further, but we think drugs were involved in his death, and Katie might have seen something she shouldn't have. So they grabbed her!"

"Who grabbed her?" Joseph asked and was getting more upset.

"We're getting close to finding that out! You tell Margaret how much or how little you want her to know. I will abide by your wishes."

"Thank you, Dave. Please keep me posted! I mean on *everything!*"

Maddy did not know anything that was going on. She just knew Jack was back on days, working somewhere in town. She had no idea where, but she really didn't care as long as he kept them supplied in food and essentials and stayed away from their daughter. She often thought of Kaitlyn, how she was doing, if she was pregnant. She needed the courage to visit with her again.

The sheriff finally located Freddy's dealer in the Santa Fe jail. He was picked up through a drug raid at a local hot spot. Taking the hour drive, the sheriff drove north to visit him. As he waited for him in one of the interrogation rooms, the inmate was finally shown in. "Cole, take a seat! Freddy Gates?"

"Yeah, I know him! What about him?"

"He was found murdered some weeks ago!"

"What the fuck! I have nothing to do with that!"

"He gets his drugs from you, *correct?*" the sheriff asked him.

"I don't know what the hell you're talking about!" Cole answered.

"Come on, Cole! I know you know he gets his coke from you!"

"Well, maybe! I direct people to where they can their fix!"

"*Stop fucking with me!*" The sheriff pounded his fist on the table. "You *are* the *one* who sells the shit!"

"Okay, you don't have to get so shitty about it! Maybe, just maybe, I sold Freddy some coke a few weeks ago. He tried to rip me off, and maybe I got a little rough! But that's all! He was breathing when I left. I swear!"

"What about this girl?" The sheriff showed him a picture of Kaitlyn O'Connor. "You ever see her at Freddy's?"

Picking up the picture and examining it closely, he said, "Nope, never seen her before! Who is she?"

"She's been missing for over a year now. We found something that places her at Freddy's."

"Whoa!" Cole said, holding up his hand. "Stop right there! I might deal in drugs here and there but have nothing to do with any kidnapping!"

"I did not say you! I'm thinking Freddy Gates!" The sheriff quickly realized that the drug dealer knew nothing as he prepared to leave. "Thanks for seeing me. I would say, don't leave town, but I guess you won't be going anywhere soon!"

"*You asshole!*" Cole shouted out as the officer took him back to his cell.

The sheriff, making it back to the precinct, informed the others about his talk with Cole, "Our drug dealer isn't going anywhere soon, so we're safe there—of him skipping town. I'm not excluding him as a suspect yet for the murder of Gates, but as for Katie, he says he's never seen her, and I believe him."

Joseph decided to tell Margaret little as possible of the conversation he and Dave had. Withholding that bit of information about the semen, he decided, was for the best. He now understood why the sheriff wanted only him there for their talk. It would have devastated her. He would keep that information to himself until it was time to let her know.

Margaret continued working in the store, greeting customers, and helping them in their needs. She even helped Teresa Gordon a few times. Teresa, since he had gone fishing with her husband, told Margaret how much fun it was. Margaret helped her purchase her own rod and reel, her own tackle box, with just as many items as her husband. Laughing, price did not matter to her!

Margaret was so happy having her friend back. Their lunches together were priceless! Together they shared many memories of Katie.

Margaret, laughing, said, "You remember her junior prom and that boy she went with? They were the strangest couple, totally opposites! She felt so sorry for him!" Both laughed.

"Yes, she asked him to go with her!" Teresa finished. "She was that way!"

"Yes, she was! She would have made a wonderful advocate."

Tears filled Margaret's eyes. Teresa stood and ran around to the other side of the booth and sat beside her friend.

Taking her in her arms, she said, "She will be! Soon she will be back home, safe in your arms!"

All the clues were starting to come together for the sheriff's department on the murder case. Fingerprints were found all over the house. Most of them belonged to Jack Hayes. That was understandable due to him being a good friend of the deceased and was always at his house. Puzzling, though, they found several prints of his on one particular window. On the glass, whole hands were all over that panel, inside and out!

Tips were coming in all the time. Some useful while several just made up with the person thinking he saw.

There was one person who knew a lot about it but was too afraid to talk. At times he would get the courage, pick up the phone to make that call, and just as he was about to punch in that final digit, he would hang up.

The owner of the house directly behind Freddy's always kept to himself. Other than arguing with Freddy about his backyard of trash, they had never met. Tanner Gibbs, the nosy backyard neighbor, spied on everyone. He was considered a recluse that no one knew anything about, but, he on the other hand, knew lots about everyone: Who was seeing who! Who was having an affair! Who was having troubles in their marriage! He would just sit on his front porch, watch all, and learn all the town's dirty secrets. He especially watched Fred Gates. He knew all about the drug dealings that went on in that house and all the visits from Jack Hayes. That was one person, though, he could not figure out—Jack Hayes! He felt something in his gut about that guy!

He did see something, something he had not shared with anyone. Along with the picture he had taken, proving it, he heard a lot of shouting and swearing that day. By sneaking over and looking through the window, he saw Jack Hayes strangle Fred Gates to death. That was when he took the picture before hurrying back to his house. Through the fence, he watched Jack drag something across the yard, something covered in a blanket. That something was the body of Freddy. The smell! That god-awful smell! A week later, another thing he saw was a person crawling through the back window; he recognized him as well. Tanner was keeping all this information to himself because he was not ready to come forward. When the state police and the sheriff's department went all over town, knocking on doors, he made them believe he was never home. Now he was ready to talk. He'd dial the number for the sheriff department, think about it, and hang up. He wasn't sure he wanted to get involved. He had to tell someone; it was eating him alive!

Tanner asked himself, "What should I do!"

The sheriff department worked endlessly at the Gates's house, hoping to find additional clues to solve the Gates's murder or Katie's clothing mystery. After finding the cocaine, it led them to believe it was a drug deal gone wrong, with Katie somehow involved. They were not ready to close that case yet: (1) where was her body? and (2) who was the killer?

Tanner finally made that call.

"Sheriff Department! How can I help you?" Joan answered.

"I need to talk to someone about the murder case?" the caller insisted.

"Hold, please, I will transfer you." Placing the call on hold, Joan rang the sheriff. "Sheriff, there is a call on line 2, stating he wants to talk to someone about the murder case."

Just as Tanner was about to hang up, the sheriff picked up, "Sheriff Thomas!"

"I know who killed Fred Gates!" Tanner blurted out.

"Hold on a minute! Who am I talking to?" the sheriff excitedly shouted out.

He stood and started waving his hand in the air to catch the attention of a deputy.

Seeing this, a deputy joined him at his side as he listened to the one-sided conversation.

"Can we meet and talk?"

"I don't know! I'm afraid!" the caller answered.

"Okay, you name the place."

"Not in town where people can see me. How about in the Sandia Mountains Park? It's far enough away, but close enough to drive."

"That's fine with me. You name the time *today!*"

"Okay! Six o'clock! Entrance 1 in the picnic area. Come alone!"

"Will do! You *will* be there?"

"Yes, I'll be there! I've kept this to myself too long!" Tanner hung up the phone.

The sheriff immediately ordered two of his deputies, "I'm meeting what I hope is a witness for the Gates murder. I'm supposed to go alone, but I want you guys close by, in the park. I hope we just solved our murder case!"

Couple of hours later, at exactly six o'clock, the sheriff was waiting for his witness. While sitting on one of the picnic tables, he checked in with his men, "You see anything yet?"

He had one man outside the park entrance and the other one stationed just past the restrooms, his eyes directed toward the sheriff.

"Truck coming! A gray, older-model Dodge pickup is heading your way. I'll get it's plates," the deputy announced.

"You hear that, Greg?" the sheriff informed his other man.

"I'm on top of it! Here comes that truck!" the other deputy answered.

After pulling in the lot and parking beside the cruiser, the sheriff stepped down off the table and proceeded toward his visitor. The door opened, and it revealed his witness, Tanner Gibbs. Tanner Gibbs, in full beard and wearing his normal overalls, lived directly behind Fred Gates. A chain-link fence separated the two yards.

"Mr. Gibbs, we have tried many times to talk with you. You were never home," the sheriff informed him.

"Yes, I was! I just wasn't ready to talk to any of you. Now I am!" Tanner answered.

As they both walked toward a table, each taking a seat on separate sides of the table, they faced each other.

"Okay, you said you know the killer of Fred Gates! Let's have it?" the sheriff started his interrogation.

"I saw what I thought looked like a person dragging something out of the house."

"Who was this person?"

"Jack Hayes!"

"Jack Hayes! You sure about this? You saw him dragging something outside? Not just a bag of trash?"

"I heard a lot of yelling that day, different than usual, like angrier! It was not the normal argument between the two. More threatening! So I snuck over to a window, and this is what I saw."

He showed him the picture off his phone of Jack strangling Fred at the exact location the sheriff found the urine.

Grabbing the phone out of Tanner's hand, the sheriff examined it carefully.

"Why in hell's name didn't you come to us sooner?"

"Sheriff, I was afraid! I've heard about the fights Jack gets into. They're not pretty!"

"We can protect you! We *will* protect you!" He called his men to join them. "I'm bringing Mr. Gibbs back with me, and one of you guys drive his car back to town, park it exactly how and where he usually parks it at his house. I want everything to look normal until we make our arrest.

On the drive back to town, Tanner stated, "I'm so glad to get that off my chest, along with me seeing him crawl back into the house."

Slamming on the breaks in the car in the middle of the road, the sheriff turned to face his passenger, "Say what? What did you just say, you saw someone crawl into the house through a window?"

"Yes, I saw Jack Hayes crawl in, then out, just as you were searching the house."

"Let's get you back into town, and *you* tell me *everything you know!*"

Back in town the sheriff hurriedly took Tanner Gibbs straight inside the precinct and put him in one of the interrogation rooms.

Tanner walked all around the room like a caged animal. He was still unsure that he was doing the right thing. He knew how angry Jack Hayes could get and how dirty he fought. Jack was always the last man standing!

A knock came at the door, and the sheriff joined Tanner. With pen and notebook in hand, the sheriff was ready for answers. He handed Tanner a soda, hoping it would calm his nerves before he started his questions. With years of experience in interrogations, the sheriff knew he had to treat this one ever so delicately.

"Tanner, I want you to tell me everything you know."

After taking a big drink from the can, he set it down and started, "I have always watched the goin's on at that house! The things I saw…"

Tanner described everything that went on in Fred Gates's house, especially the drug deals! One day he heard a loud commotion going on and saw a man, who Tanner thought to be Gates's dealer, punch Gates in the stomach and point a gun in his face. He heard Gates begging for his life until he finally handed over some money. The man then just shoved him away, took his money, and stalked out.

"Can you describe this guy for me?" the sheriff asked.

"Yes, he was probably six feet, five inches and weighed 180, 200 pounds," Tanner answered. "Now, do I have to worry about him coming after me?" Tanner asked, afraid for his life.

The man Tanner described was the guy being held in the Santa Fe jail. "No, you have nothing to worry about. That guy is in jail and probably won't be out for at least fifteen years."

This story confirmed what Cole had told him in Santa Fe, and the sheriff was able to remove his name from the suspect list. He would just let the DEA know of his drug dealings in Albuquerque.

The sheriff finished their interview and hoped he got all the information needed to arrest Jack Hayes for the murder of Fred Gates. Securing a room for him at the local hotel, Dave ordered Tanner, under no circumstance, to leave the room or make any phone calls until he heard back from him. Then Dave placed a deputy outside the door.

"Do not leave this spot! Not even for a second! I want someone here, guarding Tanner Gibbs, twenty-four hours straight until I can pick up Jack Hayes."

The sheriff ended his day by calling the prosecutor to get a warrant.

CHAPTER 19

The Shooting

Katie was working at the window every day and night while Jack was away. She was getting so close! She could now get all her fingers under the window frame. She grabbed hold with both hands and jerked hard, hoping it would break lose. It happened! As she pulled with all her might, the window broke away from its frame, causing her to fall off her chair to the ground. Glass scattered all over her. Surprisingly, she got just a few minor cuts. Her heart was racing! Before climbing out the window, she went to her baby's grave.

"Baby girl, I will be back and take you home. I love you!" she promised.

Climbing back on the chair, she was able to pull herself up. Smelling fresh air, the first time in over a year, she dragged herself through the window and was soon laying on the hard ground. Getting to her feet, she looked over the area and saw a house ahead. She slowly walked toward it. Not seeing a car, she hoped that meant Jack was gone. Seeing a back door, she cautiously entered.

Jackie, who was sitting on the sofa playing with her doll, heard a noise and looked up and saw Katie.

"*Momma, momma! Come quick!*" Maddy came out of her bedroom to see why her daughter was so distressed. "*Momma, look!*" Jackie cried, pointing toward Katie who was standing in the kitchen.

"Kaitlyn!" Maddy said and rushed to her and wrapped her arms around her. "How? What?" she asked as she held her tight.

Watching the embrace, Jackie jumped off the sofa and joined in the hug.

"We've got to get out of here. Jack will be home soon," Maddy warned them.

At that moment Jack walked through the door. "Well! Well! What have we here?"

During all the commotion, no one heard a car drive up. Shocked, they looked up and saw Jack standing before them.

"Jackie, run to your room!"

Doing as told, she ran into her room and closed the door.

"What the *hell* are you doing in here?" Jack asked, grabbing Katie by the hair and pulling her away from Maddy. He slapped her so hard he busted her lip and knocked her unconscious to the floor. "*Maddy! Maddy! What have you done now?*" Jack grabbed her next and, out of control, began hitting her with his fist in great force.

Jackie opened her door and saw her father hitting her mother.

She ran from her room, screaming, "Daddy, please stop!"

Jack shoved his daughter away.

"I'll deal with you next!" he said as he continued in full rage, beating Maddy senseless.

Jackie saw her daddy's gun, the butt sticking outside his back pocket and grabbed it.

As she pointed it at her father, she repeated, "*Daddy, stop!*"

Jack released Maddy, and she crumbled to the floor. Turning to confront his daughter, he saw the gun in her hand.

"Jackie, baby, put that gun down. Mommy and Daddy are just talking," Jack said to her, his voice gentler.

"No, you're not! You're hurting Mommy again!"

Katie was slowly awakening, trying to focus.

"Jackie honey, don't…"

Laughing, Jack held out his hand to take the gun. Jackie stepped further away from his grip.

"Give me the gun!" he demanded as he grabbed at her.

Jackie, closing her eyes, pulled the trigger. A blast echoed in the room.

Jack, stunned at what just happened, felt pain in his shoulder, with blood covering his shirt.

"*You bitch!*" he screamed, lunging at her.

Again, Jackie pulled the trigger. This time the bullet hit him in the chest.

Falling backward, he was dead before hitting the floor.

Maddy ran to her daughter and, with Katie crawling to join them, took the gun from Jackie's hand.

While they were all in a hug, the front door burst open with the sheriff rushing in, his gun drawn. Deputies came in through the back. The sheriff, seeing all that was before him, holstered his gun. Kneeling to check Jack's pulse, he knew immediately he was deceased.

Next he focused on the group of women; not believing his eyes, he yelled, "*Katie!*"

She ran into his arms, crying. This time they were happy ones!

His deputies took control of the situation. First they searched the additional rooms in the house, then outside and the surrounding premises. Finding no one else, a deputy then made the call to the coroner.

The sheriff wrapped all three women in blankets and led them out to his squad car.

Maddy held tightly on to her little girl, knowing what she just did.

"What am I gonna do?" asked Maddy.

Katie took her hand and said, "We'll get through this together! Day by day."

At the police station, Dave Thomas talked with Maddy and Katie separately. Taking Katie to a private room, first after giving her a hug, he then began his questioning.

"Katie, I can't believe I have you sitting here in my office, safe. After we're done talking, I will contact your parents and have them come in. They have never given up hope. Later we'll have to talk about you, but first I need to know what happened today. The only question I have is, who shot Jack Hayes?"

Katie, still shaking from what had transpired before her, said, "Jackie shot her father. Let me start from the beginning. I was finally able to escape what I will describe as my dungeon and enter the house. I had contact with both Maddy and Jackie until Jack found out Maddy was talking with me. Well, you can probably imagine how he felt about that. He beat me, and I can only imagine what he did to her. Then only Jackie would visit. Maddy was too afraid to get out after that. We all were clinging together and planning our escape. We didn't hear Jack come in. He saw us together and just…lost control. First he hit me, knocking me to the floor, unconscious. As I was awakening, I saw Jackie holding the gun on Jack. I saw him lunge at her, trying to get it, causing her shoot, hitting him in the shoulder. That really made him mad, and as he rushed toward her, she shot again. This time he fell back on the floor, I guess dead!"

"But you were holding the gun," the sheriff said quickly.

"Yes, after it was all done, Maddy ran to Jackie, and I crawled to join them, taking the gun out of her hands. Mr. Thomas, it was in self-defense! I swear to God!"

Seeing the condition of all three women, he knew this was true.

Taking her hands into his, he said, "I believe you, Katie. Now let's contact your parents and give them the good news."

The sheriff talked with Maddy next. While she held her sleeping daughter, she told her story, totally different than what Katie had said.

"I was so tired of Jack beating on me. I was afraid he'd start on Jackie next…" Maddy began. "I knew where Jack kept his gun…and I just shot him."

"When did Katie enter into the equation?" the sheriff asked her.

"I don't remember. I know Jack had a girl hidden out here but didn't know who. She just showed up in the house after it was all over," Maddy said and started to cry.

The sheriff sat down on the sofa beside her and said, "Maddy, come on, you know it didn't happen that way. Katie told me everything."

"No! She's lying! My little girl didn't shoot the gun."

"How do you know Katie said Jackie shot Jack?"

Looking at the sheriff, Maddy felt beaten.

"Please, my baby only did it to save her momma. Don't take her away from me!" Maddy pleaded.

"Nothing is gonna happen to you or your little girl, or even Katie. You are all safe now!"

Maddy pulled her daughter closer to her chest, realizing it was all over!

"I still have to talk with Jackie, of course, with your permission. It can be held off for a couple weeks while we review the crime scene."

At last he could make that overdue call he had been praying every day to do. Disappearing last July and back home the following year in August. Home, safe and alive!

"Joseph, can you come into the precinct right away? Bring Margaret with you."

"Dave, have you got some news?"

"Yes! No time to explain, just come!"

CHAPTER 20

Free

Joseph and Margaret entered through the station doors seeing tears in everyone's eyes.

Frightened of what they were about to hear, they held hands while they waited in the lobby.

After a few minutes, Joan greeted them, "The sheriff is waiting for you in the conference room. Please follow me!"

Opening the door to allow them to enter, she gently closed the door and continued to cry. The O'Connors saw only the sheriff and waited for what they thought was going to be bad news.

"Mom! Dad! I'm home!" Katie cried out.

Margaret, seeing her daughter, screamed out loud and ran to embrace her. Holding her tight in her arms, she cried uncontrollably.

Joseph called out, "Katie, is it really you?"

"Yes, Daddy, it is me!" she said as he joined his wife in their group hug.

The sheriff left the room, giving them some time alone. There would be plenty of time later to talk. As he went to join his staff in the lobby, they all stood and began clapping for their leader.

Holding up his hand to stop them, he said, "We all did it! Congrats to all of us for solving both cases, finding Kaitlyn O'Connor alive and Fred Gates's killer! I know we didn't get a confession, but all the evidence leads back to Jack Hayes. With that neighbor finally coming forward and telling us what he saw that day, and with the picture he had taken, the deal was sealed!"

Maddy was waiting in another room for the sheriff to return. On the sofa Jackie laid fast asleep in her mother's arms. After her continuous crying, she had finally fallen asleep. Maddy just sat there, singing and rocking her little girl back and forth.

After giving her statement of what really happened that dreadful afternoon, Maddy was finally released to go to a hotel, which the sheriff had gotten for her to stay at for a few weeks. The sheriff still had lots of questions that needed answers, so she was far from being done. He had to talk with Jackie too. They were not allowed to go back to their house, even to pick up a few things, until the investigation was over, of which she was told could go on for months. Deep down, Maddy did not ever want to go back. But she had no idea what was in her future once everything was completed, where to live and how she and Jackie would survive. She even took back her full name of Madeline Moore. She did not want to hear the name Maddy Hayes ever again.

Margaret, having not met Madeline but heard some of the details of the poor woman's life, wanted to help. She bought Jackie and her mother all the needed items a woman and little girl would need—from shampoo, bubble bath, hairbrushes, and combs to books and toys for Jackie. She also set up an account at the local department store for them to buy clothing and shoes. She wanted so desperately to meet Jackie, the little girl who was brave enough to be a friend to Katie. Even though she knew how the little one had helped her father grab Katie, Margaret felt deep in her heart that Jackie was also a victim.

Margaret and Teresa organized benefits with their church: bake sales, rummage sales, and many other ways to collect money for the Hayes women. Madeline, when living out of town with Jack, was not allowed to correspond with any of the women in town. She did not realize what friends she would soon acquire.

With the murder of Fred Gates solved, the sheriff department now dedicated all their time at the Hayes property. Per doctor's orders, the officers were not yet allowed to speak with Kaitlyn about her time with Jack. She was not in any condition to talk, so the department went about their investigation without any guidance. As they searched all through the house, they found nothing pertaining to Kaitlyn. Their search continued to the grounds that surrounded the house. As he walked the whole yard, one of the deputies came upon doors that led down into the ground.

"Sheriff, I think I found something," he radioed to his boss.

The sheriff and deputy walked all around the area and found a hole where a window was broken out. Kneeling down, the sheriff saw what he thought was a room.

"Goddamn, here is where Katie was kept!"

Opening the double doors, they walked down steps that were made from stones and covered by dirt and cobwebs and come to another door, which was locked. Having the lock cut off, they all entered, and what they found shocked them all: a tiny room containing only a dirty cot, a little sink, and one small heater. Seeing the broken window on the ground helped the sheriff understand how

Katie was able to escape. The chain lying on the ground beside a post told him she must have been chained like a dog. As he walked the area, he also found the nasty white bucket, which he quickly realized what it was used for.

"That poor girl. I cannot image what she went through this past year."

An officer took pictures inside the room while another took pictures above ground, surrounding the cellar. The area around the house had already been taped off when the women were found, but after finding the cellar, it also had to be included for the investigation.

Two weeks later, after a much-needed rest, Katie could not wait to bring her baby home to rest in peace! Keeping it to herself, she had not said anything to anybody about her buried child. She had hidden her far back in the cellar, not wanting Jack to ever find her. Even the officers did not know of her existence. She confronted the sheriff, telling him of this withheld information. Shocked at what he heard, the sheriff took Katie and her parents back to her house of horror to collect her child's body. She was told not to touch anything else. This she did not care. She only wanted her baby girl.

As they drove past the house toward the root cellar, Katie took in all the sights of where she was kept for over a year: mountains in the background surrounded by miles and miles of desert. Passing the rundown house, she thought about Jackie having to live in that house, and yet she was such a cheerful little girl. They had to park the car at a distance from the root cellar due to the staked area. With the sheriff leading the way, the closer they got to the cellar, the slower Katie walked, holding tight to her mother's hand. She squeezed tighter as they descended the stairs. Entering through the door, it reminded her of the hell she had gone through in that well-hidden room. Her parents were horrified, seeing the conditions of how their daughter had to live: the chain and shackle on the post, the nasty cot where she slept, and the bucket she had to use. Margaret thought of the miscarriage her daughter had to go through all alone, bringing tears to her eyes. Katie took the sheriff to a far, dark corner of the room. She showed him where she buried her child. She had hidden her so well no one would have ever found her. Taking the handmade casket, they left the premises. She never wanted to see that place ever again.

Making a drive to the Santa Fe Health Department, she had to record what she could remember of the birth and death of her baby girl. They were concerned why she had not come forward earlier about the death of her baby, but the sheriff shut that conversation down right away. After talking with the coroner, Katie was finally allowed to take home and bury the body of her child. Margaret had come to love the grandchild she never got to hold.

Having a private ceremony at the Christian church where she was baptized just outside town, Katie put her baby girl, Faith, to rest. Katie and her parents were the only ones at the burial.

The time had come for Sheriff Thomas to have that long over-due talk with Jackie Hayes. With Madeline by her side, Jackie was needed to tell the story on how Katie was taken.

"Jackie," the sheriff began, "you understand the difference between telling the truth and lying?"

"Yes, Mr. Thomas. Mommy taught me never to lie. To always tell the truth."

"Good, Jackie. You understand what this meeting is about today?"

"Yes, Mommy told me to tell the truth about how I helped Daddy get Katie to our house." Jackie started to cry. "It's all my fault!"

"Please don't cry, and no, you are not responsible for that. Your daddy tricked you into getting her. Isn't that right?"

"Yes, Daddy said we were getting mommy a surprise in town. I was so excited!"

The sheriff went on, trying to calm the little girl in front of him by saying, "Yes, you keep remembering that. "You wanted to please your daddy for your mommy."

"Now, try to remember that day, a long time ago. What did your daddy want you to do?"

"We were outside the fish store, and Daddy wanted me to get Katie outside to the back. I was to run into the store, find her, and trick her into coming outside with me."

"How were you supposed to trick her?"

"I was supposed to lie," she said, looking at her mother. "Mommy, I'm sorry I lied. But Daddy made me. He slapped me to make me cry and get Katie, telling her I had a hurt puppy."

Madeline kissed her daughter's head, saying, "That's okay, baby, go ahead and tell the sheriff the rest of the story."

Jackie continued, "After he slapped me and I was crying, I ran into the store, found Katie working in front, and pulled her outside with me to the back, where Daddy was waiting."

"Where was your daddy?" the sheriff asked.

"He was hiding behind the trash cans. When I got her there, he hit her and put her in the trunk of the car, then we drove home."

"What did you do then? With Katie?"

"We drove to the root cellar, where I used to play, and he took her down the steps. He wouldn't let me go with him. Just told me to go up to the house."

Finishing her story, Jackie crawled into her mother's lap and continued to cry. Madeline also began to cry.

"Is that all, Mr. Thomas? I want to take Jackie back to the room."

"Yes, Madeline, I got all I needed. Thank you for letting me talk with her," Dave said, turning off the recorder.

"You have one brave, young lady!" the sheriff assured Madeline.

"Thank you, Sheriff Thomas. I think so too!" Madeline said before carrying Jackie, even as big as she was, back to their room to rest.

Weeks after their rescue, Madeline and her daughter still could not get any privacy. Even though they all helped, the town would still question and bother Madeline about her life. They wanted to hear all the juicy stuff Madeline had gone through.

One day, while Madeline was shopping for clothes for Jackie, the saleslady in the store interrupted her.

"Madeline, dear, how are you doing? I've got to ask, how did it make you feel, your husband having relations with another woman? Did you ever join them?" the saleslady asked.

Another lady at the post office wanted to know how Jack treated his daughter. All this shocked Madeline, and she began to just stay in the room.

Teresa heard about this going on and in church one Sunday morning told the ladies how she felt about it.

The reverend knew Teresa wanted to speak and summoned her to join him up front.

"Ladies, I am so ashamed of all of you! How could you speak to Madeline the way I've heard you all do…the questions you asked? What if it were you?" she said, pointing to one of her friends, "or you," pointing to another.

Each lady just lowered her head. Teresa stepped down from the pulpit and walked out as she looked straight ahead, not acknowledging anyone.

Teresa took Madeline and Jackie away from all that by taking them to her home, away from the meddling people, so they could heal.

Night after night Jackie would wake in the middle of the night, screaming out, "*Daddy, no! Don't hurt Mommy!*" Several times in the night she'd wake in a cold sweat.

Madeline would run into the room to calm her daughter and finally just started sleeping with her. She could feel Jackie sob and thrust back and forth in her sleep every night. The Gordons found the perfect psychiatrist to help the young girl cope with her ghosts. Madeline was so thankful to find such a friend in Teresa.

Teresa also helped Madeline get Jackie enrolled in the local school and was to start in a few weeks. Teresa had to explain the situation of Jackie's mental health, and she was able to get the school's approval for her late start. Things would be calmer around town by then.

Madeline had no luck in locating her parents. No one knew where they moved. She took a job with the Gordons as a housekeeper. Teresa soon learned how good Madeline was as a seamstress and urged her to start her own business. Madeline was always having to mend and make hers and Jackie's clothes at home and found how much she loved sewing. Teresa helped in the advertising of Madeline's talent by making flyers and placed them all over town. She also set up a website, displaying pictures of dresses for all to see. When Teresa loaned her a small amount of cash, Madeline was able to purchase a sewing machine, cutting table, and other supplies needed to start her business. She was soon up and running, with orders coming in. Maddy was on her way to making a living! Madeline was able to pay back the money Teresa had loaned to her very quickly.

She and Jackie were soon ready to move into their own place. The house where she lived with Jack was bulldozed down, and the root cellar was filled in with dirt. They both no longer existed. She wanted no reminder of ever living there, so she put the land up for sale. It sold quickly and gave Madeline cash for the purchase of her new place. Very excited, she was able to find a small house in town, next to Jackie's school. Teresa and Margaret, both with different styles of decorating, gave Madeline ideas for each room. Hearing their ideas, she boldly told them, "No!" without thinking. She waited for that slap to come when she disobeyed Jack. It never came. The ladies applauded her, clapping their hands together.

Teresa, with her children all grown and living so far away, treated Madeline like a daughter. The women in town accepted Madeline and stopped meddling and started taking all their mending to her. The best news in Madeline's life was that Jackie was sleeping better and all through the night. She was able to be a little girl again, going to school and making friends. Jackie loved her school and very quickly caught up with the class in their studies.

After several months, the sheriff felt it time to confront Katie about her experience. He understood that she would be more comfortable at home, so he met her there. Margaret met him at the door and showed him to the study. Katie was already waiting; she knew what the visit was about. It was time to give her story, her year of hell! She had not said a word to anyone, including her mother. Until today! Margaret did not know everything that her daughter had gone through. She only saw the room where she stayed and the conditions in which she had to live. To have Katie talk about her past year, she hoped it would help her to heal. What Margaret was about to hear was worse than she had ever dreamed—what her sweet girl had gone through.

The sheriff, in a chair across from the sofa on which Katie and her mother sat, turned on the small recorder and began.

"Katie, you know why I'm here today. You need to take us back to that day, the day you were taken! I know it will be difficult. Do you want your mother to leave the room while we talk?" the sheriff asked compassionately.

"No, she can stay."

Margaret took hold of her hand.

"Anytime you need a break, please feel free to ask. We'll try to get through this the best we can."

On the sofa, Katie had a death grip on a chain in her hand. It held the spoon that helped her escape. She had made it into a necklace and wore it around her neck. Since coming home, it had not left her body.

Katie began her story:

"That Friday I was working the front register when Jackie came running in, all upset and crying. She was telling me something about a puppy, it being hurt or something. She pulled me around to the back of the store, and just as I was about to ask her where it was...the last thing I remember was her saying she was sorry! I woke, finding myself in that dark room!"

Margaret pulled her daughter closer.

"I recognized him right away from one day when he came into the store drunk. Dad made him leave right away. I never did know what his name was. The couple of times I got to talk with his wife, I can't remember if I ever heard his name. I didn't even know her name until we got rescued.

"That first night he raped me!" Margaret was in tears. Katie herself also started to cry. "It was my first time! Mommy, my first time! Charlie always wanted to, but I held onto my faith. Mommy, the things he made me do! I am so ashamed!" she cried, burying her face into her momma's arms.

"Let's take a quick break," the sheriff broke in, pausing the recorder. "Margaret, could you bring us something cold to drink, please?"

"Yes, Dave."

Giving her daughter a squeeze, she left to get the drinks.

"Katie, do you still want your mother here while you continue your story? I'm sorry that I am making you relive that horror. But I've got to know."

"Yes, I understand! I've got to talk about it, and yes, I need her here! She's giving me the courage to do this. They both saw how I lived. This will close my past so I can open my future!"

Margaret reentered the room, bringing in the beverages as the sheriff pushed *Record* again.

"My clothes were so ripped they barely covered me. One afternoon he came in, carrying bags, bags from our store, with clothing… from our store! I knew he was a horrible man…but that was the worst thing he could have done!"

"I remember that day, honey. I am so sorry… I helped her pick out those things. His wife told me they were for her. She was trying to lose weight. It didn't make sense at the time, but people are funny at times. That poor woman was so scared! I told your dad she was afraid to make a move without his permission. She was probably bullied in to going shopping with him. I'm so sorry, sweetheart. The gall of that man to come face-to-face with us and he having you held as a captive!"

"Yes, Margaret, Joseph was right on target about Jack Hayes. I just didn't see it. We didn't have any actual proof to bring him in anyway. He was always one step ahead of us."

"I started working on that window, digging around the sill. It was my hope of escape. At first, I only had a little nail to work with. Then one time, after he dropped off my meal, he always took back with him the dishes and eating utensils, but that one time he was mad and did not stay and eat with me. He just left all the dishes and left. I never got to have a fork, but I took that spoon and hid it from him when he came back and took the dishes. He must have not paid attention, not getting the spoon. Anyway, I was able to do faster work with that spoon, even though the nail was sharper.

"I'd work at that window anytime he was gone. Working around that cold window, I started to feel sick. I thought I got the flu or something. I'd wake up feeling nauseous and throw up. I felt tired all the time."

Margaret, tears forming, held her breath; she knew where her daughter was going. Tightening her grip on Katie's hand, she braced herself for what was coming.

The sheriff also knew where this talk was going.

"Let's take another break, to stretch our legs," he said, turning off the recorder.

He stepped outside to let Margaret get ahold of herself for her daughter's sake. Ten minutes later, he pushed *Record* again to let Katie continue her story.

"It didn't even dawn on me about being pregnant. I didn't even realize I missed any periods. He was emptying my bucket that one time, and he stormed back in and asked me. He was mad at me for throwing up all the time. He didn't come back for several days. I was so hungry!

"He'd come back lots of times after that, so drunk, and be so rough with me. I can't believe I didn't lose the baby then. He also forgot to reattach the chain to my ankle, which was a blessing.

"I tried to keep track of time by scratching marks on the wall. I know I missed my birthday, Thanksgiving, and Christmas. As my belly grew rounder, it really made him mad, and he'd make me sleep on the ground. That terrible day came when he threw me against the wall, hit me with his fists, then kicked me until I passed out." Katie cried in her mother's arms. "He made me lose my baby! I buried my little girl!"

Another break was taken; the sheriff left the room, tears in his eyes.

Katie finalized her story by telling of her escape.

"The rest you have in my statement, the day we were rescued."

The sheriff turned off the recorder, collected his things, and prepared to leave.

"Thank you, young lady, you are one hell of a survivor!" he said, giving them both a hug and left.

Katie stayed at home for months, afraid to face anyone. She just stayed in the house, in her room. A few times she would venture into the kitchen to join her mother but never went outside. A complete physical examination was given, finding no permanent damage, and all the bruises were slowly fading. Her mental state was the worst. Her ordeal made her afraid of men, afraid of the dark, afraid of everything! Margaret was told it could take years for Katie to face her fears. The nightmares still woke her. Margaret tried sleeping with her as a comfort but soon learned that was worse for Katie. It reminded her of Jack and his ways. So instead, Margaret sat in a chair, close as Katie would allow, and watched her daughter sleep.

Many of the O'Connors' closest friends wanted to help, but Katie wanted nothing to do with anyone. She was not ready. Katie's friends, who had gone on to college, would stop by to see her on the weekends, but she would not see them! Charlie stopped by a couple of times, but Katie would tell her mom to send him away too. They all stopped coming around and went their separate ways. Everyone wanted back the girl who loved people. The only person she had any correspondence with was Jackie Hayes. Teresa would bring her out to the O'Connors to visit weekly, only Jackie; Madeline was never invited. They would sit for hours, laughing and talking about Jackie's day at school. Margaret and Teresa would sit back and watch Katie come alive when she was with that girl. Jackie would excitedly tell Katie what went on each day, all the funny things that happened in school. She also let Katie in on a secret about a boy she liked and hoped liked her, giggling.

That September Katie was home for her twentieth birthday. No party was planned. She still would not talk with anyone except Jackie. Margaret did not care about having a party; she was happy to have her daughter home. But she constantly worried about her. Katie would jump at any noise and still would not let anyone touch her, only allowing her mother to come close. She finally began to let her mother kiss her before bed—no one else! If her father approached her too fast, she would crumple down to the floor and cry out. Seeing this hurt him terribly; he tried to understand. The psychiatrists said it could take her a long time for her to trust any man. Jack Hayes had broken her down!

Madeline was able to purchase an already-decorated cake for Jackie this year for her birthday. Twelve candles displayed on top and were waiting to be blown out by the birthday girl. Teresa was the only guest who attended the small party, carrying a handful of gifts. She had gotten so close to the little girl.

Teresa became the grandmother Jackie never got to meet. She would take her along with her on errands while Madeline worked in her shop. Every day Jackie came home with something new. One evening she came home with a small kitten. Hugging it close, she loved that kitten, never letting it out of her sight.

Christmas was a happier time. Katie was slowly coming back to life. As gifts were exchanged, Katie, with her bright smile, joined in all the fun. As she was starting to trust her father, she finally let him kiss her. That was the best gift of all, his daughter's kiss. But still no hug! She still would not allow him to embrace her. Her father, full of hope, knew that a hug was coming soon. She still needed a light on in her room but was sleeping better. It was a wonderful Christmas.

Christmastime for Jackie was unbelievable. Since they now live in town, Jackie was able to see how the town came alive in color. Businesses were decorated with thousands of twinkle lights. An enormous Christmas tree was displayed in the park for all to enjoy. Jackie thought it is was so beautiful and could not stop looking at it. Jackie joined the carolers as they sang Christmas songs in the evenings.

Madeline bought a live tree and decorated it herself after Jackie had gone to bed on Christmas Eve. She could not wait to see Jackie's face when she woke up. With Teresa's help, she bought toys and other things a little girl might want. This time she was able to buy brand-new books, not like the used ones she had gotten through the book club.

Teresa pulled Jackie to the side and asked her if she wanted to get something for her mother for Christmas. She never heard of doing something like that before. Teresa, after telling Madeline she was taking Jackie out for a while, took her to the department store and explained how to shop. Jackie, so excited, went from one department to another, looking for that perfect gift. She finally settled on a beautiful picture frame. She knew what picture she was going to use. Looking through her mother's things one day, she came across a picture of her mother and herself sitting on a porch swing. It must have been taken when they first moved out to their place. Her mother used to tell her stories about how happy they were when they first moved there. She said it was before her daddy got sick. Teresa helped her purchase the frame and dig out the picture out of boxes. Her mother said at first she did not want anything from their old house but decided later she wanted her box of pictures that she had saved of all her family.

That Christmas morning was the start of their new life. Jackie loved all her presents her mother had gotten for her. She especially loved the collection of books that her mother picked out for her. *The Princess Diaries, Harriet the Spy*, and *Beezus and Ramona* were just a few of the books Madeline picked up.

When Madeline opened her gift, she saw a beautiful picture frame. When she revealed the picture, tears filled her eyes. She always loved that picture, her and her daughter, three years old at the time, swinging on the porch swing. Jack had taken that picture when life was good.

It was the first of many Christmases that would come.

Margaret still had not returned to work. She enjoyed staying home with Katie, keeping her company, which Katie also enjoyed.

Every day customers asked Joseph how Katie was doing. They, too, cared! Joseph enjoyed telling them how much she was improving each day.

"It won't be long. Katie will be back here, working beside her mom."

CHAPTER 21

Happily Ever After

The new year had come, spring, summer, and fall. It was again September, and Katie's twenty-first birthday was around the corner. A celebration this time! This year there would be a party! But still the only guest invited was Jackie Hayes. She heard that Jackie had never had her own birthday party. This gave Katie an idea.

"Mom, I want to give Jackie a birthday party! I want to find out when it is and give her the best party ever!" Katie told Margaret.

"Of course! What a wonderful idea! I'll have Teresa help plan it."

"Yes, we will have the biggest party and invite all her friends from school." Katie laughed.

Margaret, hearing the laughter and seeing the excitement on her daughter's face, spoke to herself, "I don't care what it costs if that's what it takes to bring my girl back to us!"

What Teresa found out was, Jackie's thirteenth birthday was the following month in October.

"Perfect! We will make it a Halloween party: costumes, carved pumpkins, all the works!" Katie said, all excited.

She had her mom get a list of Jackie's classmates, including Luke, the boy she liked. It was decided to have the party in the middle of the month and, after getting her dad's permission, have it in the store's warehouse. Two weeks later, Katie rode with her mother into town, her first time out of the house since her return, to shop for decorations, order a cake, and set up arrangements for all the children to pick out costumes. All were told *not* to say a word to Jackie. It was to be a surprise!

Finishing the decorating, Katie was ready. Margaret and Joseph were excited for their daughter to be out in the world again.

The day of the party, Teresa brought both Jackie and Madeline out to the O'Connors'. Madeline, knowing of the surprise, was touched by what was about to occur. Halloween was one day she never dwelled upon, so close after her daughter's birthday of October 25. Of course, at school little treats were given out, but no costumes were worn. This was a first for them both. All the ladies were dressed up: a witch, a mummy, a queen. Seeing them all made Jackie cry out in laughter. When she saw her own outfit, it brought her to tears: a fairy princess! It was the most-beautiful dress she had ever seen. After fixing her hair, Katie placed a tiara upon her head.

"You ready to go?" she asked.

"Oh, yes!"

Holding hands, they both climbed into the back seat of the car. Madeline sat in the front seat beside Margaret as they drove off. Teresa left earlier to greet the guests and hide with them.

The party was perfect! Jackie finally got the birthday of her dreams! Presents. Cake. Games. Even dancing! She got to dance with Luke!

Margaret stood with Teresa behind the cake, serving large pieces, while Maddy filled cups with punch.

"I think I have my little girl back!" Margaret informed her friend.

"Yes, I think you do! Look how she acts around the little ones. Teaching might be another fine choice for her."

Joseph peeked inside the room; orange and black colors filled the room, along with loud music. He watched his daughter enjoying herself, the first time in over a year. Bringing tears to his eyes, he waved to his wife and blew her a kiss.

After the party, Katie started going into town more and more. She always stopped first at her baby's grave and left flowers each time.

Making a stop at her father's store, Katie greeted all her friends. She was becoming a regular in town these days. She saw all the changes her mother had made and agreed with her father that her mother was a genius! The added clothing, the different-colored rods and reels! She laughed when she saw the purple-and-pink tackle boxes. They were no longer just a men's store with men's merchandise but now a family store for the complete family.

One night at supper, Katie brought up the subject of college.

"Do you think they still have my application on file?"

Stunned, Margaret answered, "I'm not sure. We can certainly call first thing in the morning."

"I see how Jackie is adapting to her new life. I want to do something with mine," Katie admitted.

"Darling, that would be wonderful! Remember how much you liked helping others. It is in your blood!" her mother reminded her.

"Thank you so much Ms. Brooks, yes we can be there 8:00 Monday morning," Margaret happily told the school representative.

"Mother, is it true? I can really go?" Katie had listened in on the conversation.

"Yes, you can. Monday you just need to reapply and select your classes. I had to explain what happened…" Seeing her daughter's face, Margaret stopped talking. "Honey, don't be ashamed! Be proud! You are a survivor!"

Katie agreed with her mother, "Yes, I did survive, and I'm going to hold my head up high!"

"So does that mean we're going shopping? New clothes, school supplies. Your dad is going to flip out!" Margaret said as they both laughed. "You'll need to start packing! Santa Fe, here we come!"

As soon as she said those words, Margaret turned white as a sheet!

"Mom, what's wrong?"

Concerned, Katie saw fright in her mother's face.

"It just came to me! You'll be leaving us…again! When we just got you back!" Margaret replied.

"But, Mom, this time I can come home, or you can come up and visit anytime!" Katie said, easing her mother's pain.

N.C. Jones is just a country girl born and raised in Indiana. She enjoys reading and spending time with her family. She and her husband love to travel on their Harley.

CPSIA information can be obtained
at www.ICGtesting.com
Printed in the USA
LVHW021117200121
676961LV00003B/222

9 781662 418013